IN THE MURDERER'S BRAIN
THE COMPLETE CASES OF THE
SCIENTIFIC CLUB, VOLUME 3

IN THE MURDERER'S BRAIN

THE COMPLETE CASES OF THE SCIENTIFIC CLUB, VOLUME 3

RAY CUMMINGS

ILLUSTRATED BY

**JOSEPH A. FARREN
FRANK R. PAUL
AMOS SEWELL
RAYMOND WARDELL**

POPULAR PUBLICATIONS · 2025

TABLE OF CONTENTS

MEMORIES OF GUILT

1

"**IT MAY HAVE** been an accident," said the Doctor, "but, gentlemen, we do not think so. The probability is it was suicide—or murder."

"What did you say her name was?" the Chemist asked.

"Anita Paolino—a girl of Spanish parentage, born here in New York."

The Doctor gazed around this private room of the Scientific Club in which a few of his fellow club members were gathered. "If it were a suicide, gentlemen, there is nothing to be done. But Detective Marberry thinks there is a reasonable chance it was murder. In which case—"

"Found floating in the river, you said," interrupted the Banker.

"In the Narrows, off Staten Island. The circumstances are simple. Altogether too simple, in fact. A murder devoid of complicating circumstances is usually the most difficult of all to solve. A bizarre, involved crime is generally quite easy.

"If you push your victim off a dock—using no weapon—leaving no evidence of the time or the location of the murder—and particularly if you have no specific motive—or perhaps a motive held in common by several other people—then, gentlemen, you are reasonably safe from detection."

"Did this girl get pushed off a dock?" asked the Astronomer.

The Doctor shrugged. "We have, as yet, no idea. Here is the sum total of our knowledge—and I think you will admit it gives little basis for routine detective work. Last week the body of a young girl was found in the Narrows. It had been in the water rather a long time—just how long, there was no way of telling with any exactitude. No marks of violence upon it—and the autopsy showed death by drowning.

"In the morgue it was identified as the body of Anita Paolino—identified and claimed by the father and mother. Anita had disappeared on January 4th last. She was fifteen years old—a small, very pretty, dark-haired girl. She lived with her parents—Spanish, but they lived in the Italian colony near Stapleton, Anita was one month under sixteen. A Spanish girl matures very young. She looked fully eighteen.

"About five o'clock on the afternoon of the 4th, Anita took a five-dollar bill and started for the grocery nearby. She did not return—nor did she ever get to the grocery. No one could be located who had seen her. No slightest clue, until her body was found in the Narrows.

"Her parents say that at the time of her disappearance she seemed in good health, though they had noticed and been puzzled that apparently she was depressed and unhappy for a week or two past.

"The condition of the body would indicate that she had been drowned on the 4th, 5th, or 6th of January. The autopsy revealed perhaps the most common motive for this type of tragedy—she was to become a mother—a fact unknown to her parents. Hardly an accidental death, therefore. Most likely a suicide, or a murder.

"It's a lie, I tell you!" He stood trembling, gripping the back of his chair.

"No clues at all, gentlemen. Assume it was murder. We can't tell where it was committed, or when. The motive is clear—yet it is a motive any one of a number of persons could have possessed. The girl—so far as her parents believed—was a good girl. Gentle, sweet, obedient—gave them no trouble.

"She was remarkably pretty, and popular. She knew and liked many young men—of both Spanish and Italian families. But her parents can name only two whom she seemed particularly to favor. Both are Spanish—by name Ramón Gutierrez, age eighteen, and Julio Salta, age nineteen.

"Anita's parents liked them both—thought possibly she might ultimately marry one of them. Both were young men of good reputation, good family—in school still and with no business prospects, no reasonable prospect of marrying for some years."

The Doctor's face was solemn, his voice earnest as he went on: "If we are to assume murder, gentlemen, we can only reason that the greatest probability lies with one of these two young men. A pathetic sort of thing, isn't it? Three respectable, hard-working families—with youth to bring tragedy upon them.

"The appalling youth of it! A girl of fifteen, young men of eighteen and nineteen. No vicious, depraved criminal in this—only youth, inexperienced, heedless of consequences."

The Lawyer said: "Is there any choice between these two young men?"

"No. We can find no choice. One small detail I haven't mentioned. The girl had a gold locket; in it she carried a tiny picture of each of them. The locket was on her when she disappeared; it was still on her when her body was found. The pictures were wet, but both easily recognizable.

"The parents can remember no preference for either of the young men—the parents did not dream there was anything serious at all. The girl—since she did have some secret attachment—may easily be imagined hiding it with an outward careful impartiality.

"Marberry has, of course, investigated the whereabouts of Ramón Gutierrez and Julio Salta during the days in question. We believe that Anita met her death on January 4th, 5th, or 6th. I need not go into details concerning the proven movements of the lads over this period.

"Both live at home in Stapleton with their parents. On January 4th neither showed any unusual absence from home. For the 5th, Ramón's movements are not so well proven—and for the 6th, Julio has no witnesses to prove where he was much of the time.

"This is not unusual, of course, particularly as we cannot

altogether credit the testimony, when favorable, of the immediate families. But gentlemen, just try yourselves to give subsequent, satisfactory legal proof of your movements during any specified period of time.

"It frequently cannot be done. Yet, merely as an indication of probability, we would have to suspect Ramón more strongly of a crime committed during the evening and night of the 5th—and Julio for one committed the evening following.

"Only an indication of probability, gentlemen. Either could no doubt have had opportunity any evening and night. Yet the laws of probability are strong factors to be considered. Probable things happen much more frequently than improbable things."

"But you don't know on which night the murder was committed," the Inventor remarked.

"True. But we may be able to find out. We assume it was after dark. Also presumably during the evening, when Anita may have been lured to the water. Let us say she ran away from home, fearing exposure. Ignorance of youth— pathetic, yet so normal! Young people don't know what to do when trouble comes.

"She ran away—perhaps to hide—and get work. Or hoping the young man would marry her, and they might go away together. Conceive her hiding somewhere—perhaps with him visiting her secretly. Himself confused by this trouble—this menace fallen upon him.

"Then, one of these evenings they go out together to the waterfront somewhere, where in winter it is lonely and desolate. Fearfully, helplessly they discuss what they are to do. He knows she cannot swim. A sudden impulse—

without plan, thought, or reason—and he has removed the menace and become a murderer.

"That's about the way such things occur, gentlemen. And I honestly think one of these young men did it, on one of those evenings. In choosing the man and the evening, we have a greater probability for Ramón on the 5th, and Julio on the 6th. With no distinction between the nights except that the 5th was moonlit and the 6th heavily overcast. A detail which might be turned to advantage—"

"Frank, listen," the Banker interrupted. "You're getting altogether too delicately technical for me. Have you got some scheme for prying the truth out of one of those young men? If you have, what is it? I can't follow this hair-splitting theory on probabilities."

The Doctor smiled. "I'll be practical enough in a moment, George. Yes, I have sent for the young men. Marberry's assistant is on his way over here with them. I'm going to attempt—with Dr. Gregg's supervision—an experiment in psychology upon them—"

He indicated the Alienist who sat beside him. "Dr. Gregg thinks it possible for us to learn from the guilty one—"

"Here they are," ejaculated the Very Young Man.

2

THREE MEN ADVANCED into the room—the detective's assistant and the two suspects. As the Doctor had said, there was little to choose between the circumstances incriminating Ramón Gutierrez and Julio Salta, so indeed was their appearance quite similar. The same type exactly—slim, rather small youths, with sleek black hair, dark eyes with lashes almost girlish, and swarthy complexions.

They were well dressed—presented a dapper, jaunty aspect, which in an American would have seemed effeminate, but in them was only characteristically Latin. They were eighteen and nineteen years old, yet both looked and acted as though they were well into their twenties.

As they were being introduced to the club members, they bore themselves with a quiet, unconscious dignity. Charming manners—the type of young man who is at his best on a dance floor among a bevy of girls. Yet both were obviously nervous.

Julio, rather the larger and the better-looking of the two, lighted a brown-paper Spanish cigarette and puffed it furiously. Ramón, paler, more studious in appearance, smiled gracefully. He seemed somewhat more composed than his companion, but obviously it was only outwardly.

The Doctor placed their chairs side by side. Ramón sat down, Julio shoved his chair further away. Their glances crossed, and every man in the room was aware of a hatred smoldering between them.

The Doctor was saying: "I know that neither of you wanted to come here tonight. You both resent the grilling the authorities have put you through? But you have to submit, naturally."

His tone was not particularly friendly. They gazed at him, first with surprise, then with darkening anger. Julio said: "What is it that you want of me?" A musical voice—perfect English with that slow, careful enunciation of the foreigner, a Spanish accent and a slight Spanish twist to his phrasing.

The Doctor smiled. "You will learn in a moment." He met Ramón's antagonistic stare and added: "You have nothing to fear from us—nothing at all. For innocent young men, you have been put to a great deal of annoyance—indignity. That is unavoidable. You have conducted yourselves well—like gentlemen, both of you. And I know you will continue to do so."

"What is it that you want now?" It was Ramón who asked the question this time. "I have told all that I know. Also has Julio—"

"You take care of your own affair," Julio burst out angrily.

The Doctor raised his hand. "No quarreling, please. You were both in love with poor little Anita—and very likely each of you thinks that the other murdered her. Do you?"

He shot the sudden question. Neither answered; but their glares of hatred toward each other were answer enough.

"Murdered her," the Doctor reiterated. "Yet why should anyone murder her?"

Still no answer. A sullenness seemed to have fallen upon them. Or was it that they were intelligent enough to fear a trap—knew that their safest course lay in being silent?

Abruptly Julio said: "She loved me—not him. He was jealous. He—"

Ramón cried: "That is a lie! I was not jealous of him. She did love me and I would have married her someday. We would have planned it soon—"

The Doctor checked him. "None of that can be proven. The point is—Anita was murdered. The authorities believe you are both innocent or you would have been arrested days ago. But we do not *know* you are innocent. You are intelligent enough to understand the distinction. And until your innocence is established satisfactorily to the police, you will have to submit to investigations."

He eyed them narrowly. "On the other hand, each of you believes the other is guilty. You dislike each other. You both think there is a chance that the other may suddenly be proven guilty. That's what you are hoping now—and that's another reason why you're going to do what we tell you—now, tonight."

"What is it that you want?" Ramón repeated.

Julio looked up from the floor at his feet. "I will do what you tell me."

The Doctor relaxed. "Of course you will. Well, that's fine." He smiled a friendly smile, which both of them made a forced attempt to answer.

"A simple experiment in psychology," the Doctor went on easily. "The result of it will perhaps exonerate you both. I'm not going to explain its technicalities—you've doubtless heard of psychological tests—you know what I mean. A test of memory.

"Detective Marberry has questioned you very closely concerning what you did during the days of January 4th, 5th, and 6th. You had difficulty remembering some of your movements. Perfectly natural. If you asked me where I went and what I did two weeks ago today, I'd have trouble telling you.

"But what we want now is to discover just how normal your memory is. We want to be sure that you can remember details as well as you should. You understand me? If you prove to have normally retentive memories—why, then we will be satisfied."

The Doctor paused a moment. Both the young men seemed to be pondering his words—puzzled, and with a growing perturbation. They were intelligent youths. His explanation was far from satisfactory to them. They did not know what he meant—could not fathom the purpose in what he had just said. And the realization seemed to alarm them. Yet obviously they grasped that any sign of reluctance would be incriminating.

The Doctor repeated: "It will be best for you if your memory proves normally retentive. If I've puzzled you— just keep that one fact in mind. I'm absolutely sincere—I wouldn't like to have either of you show us that you can't remember details. Not when we've had you testify so minutely to your movements during those days. It would very largely nullify your testimony. You see that, don't you?"

They nodded dubiously.

"Quite so. To be specific then. I'm going to give you an account of what happened to Anita Paolino. Oh, yes, we know what happened! We have ways of finding out. We know all about it except, unfortunately, we do not know the guilty man. Listen closely— Dr. Gregg, may I have your memoranda?"

The Alienist handed him a paper. "Thank you. Now listen closely. Here is a brief description of the murder of Anita—exactly as it happened." He adjusted his glasses, and read very slowly:

"They went down to the shore. It was high above the water. They sat down on the bank. It was a lonely spot. It was not very dark because of the reflection of the starlight from the water. Anita said: 'I do not have to marry you.' They almost quarreled. Then he kissed her. She was toying with the chain of a little pendant she wore about her neck. She said something to him. He answered loftily: 'You can't make me believe it, my child.' Later he suddenly pushed her off the bank."

The Doctor looked up. "You hear those brief, almost unrelated facts? Well, I want you to remember them. Listen carefully—I'll read them again."

He reread the paragraph, dwelling upon each statement. The young men listened with a fascinated attentiveness. The Doctor finished the second reading and put the paper in his pocket. "You keep those facts in mind, won't you? Keep your mind on them. I don't want you to forget them." He rose to his feet. "Jack, is everything ready in there?"

The Very Young Man nodded. "Yes, sir. All ready. Who goes in first?"

The Doctor crossed to where temporary curtains enclosed a corner of the clubroom—a space some ten feet square. Within this curtained area was a table with a light above it. On the table were scattered some twenty-odd small articles: A fan, a dance card, a hoop of embroidery, a gold locket on a gold chain, a ring, a large tortoise-shell comb—all belongings of the dead girl.

The Doctor, led Ramón and Julio forward. "Anita's things. Most of them you have seen before, of course. I'm going to let you—one at a time—gaze at this table for two minutes. I want you to regard these things closely. There are twenty-four separate articles.

"You will have two minutes to look at them. When you come out, you will write a list of all of them you can remember. It is merely a memory test. If you can name between fifty and seventy-five percent of them correctly, it will answer our purpose and we will consider you normal."

"Who goes in first?" repeated the Very Young Man.

"Immaterial. You, Ramón. Go inside. We'll close the curtains. I'll call you in two minutes."

Ramón entered. The Doctor drew the curtains upon him. The Very Young Man had disappeared, but no one noticed the fact.

"Time's up," called the Doctor. He opened the curtains. Ramón came out; Julio went in.

Ramón said: "Shall I write them at once?"

"Yes. Dr. Gregg will give you paper and pencil." His watch was in his hand. "All right, Julio— Your time is up." He drew aside the curtains. Julio took a last look at the table and came out.

"Get your paper and pencil from Dr. Gregg."

Within five minutes the lists were made out. The Doctor handed them to the Alienist with whom he exchanged a sharp glance. Julio said hesitantly: "I do not know, Dr. Adams—some of these, it may be, are wrong."

"No matter," smiled the Doctor. "We only expect to get approximate results. Stay seated. Keep your pencils—here is another sheet of paper. I want you now to write down all you can remember of those facts concerning the murder. Write just what I read you a few moments ago—write it freely, just as you remember it.

"What Anita said to the young man and what he said to her. Where they went and what happened. Don't be alarmed! There's nothing to alarm you in this. Just write out approximately what I read you—no hurry, I'll give you plenty of time."

They began presently to write. The Very Young Man had reappeared. Quietly, but with an obvious excitement, he drew the Doctor aside, whispered to him.

The Doctor's expression was triumphant. "He did, Jack?"

"Yes! I saw him plainly! Smeared it with his thumb! Can you beat it?"

"Sh!"

"Yes—but listen—what about his list? He's the guilty one all right. Did you see his list yet?"

"Wait, Jack! Quiet! We'll get him in a moment!"

3

THE WRITTEN PARAGRAPHS were ready at last. The Doctor took them. He conferred with the Alienist.

Ramón said impatiently: "I have done what you ask, Dr. Adams. Is there more of this?"

"No. Not much more." Papers in hand, the Doctor rose to his feet. His face was grim, his voice tense as he swung to address the club members.

"Gentlemen, it isn't necessary for me to accuse one of these young men of murder. Their own writing speaks for itself. One of them is plainly innocent; the other one is guilty—as guilty as though he had confessed his crime to us in so many words!"

The detective had quietly edged forward. "Sit down, you!" He waved them both back to their chairs. The color had drained from their faces. One terrified by his guilt; the other frightened by the fear that he might falsely be accused.

The Doctor went on: "I need only read you what they have written, gentlemen—and every one of you will know at once who is guilty. It takes no technical skill to see it. Only common sense. Judge for yourselves. Here is the original paragraph I read them. Hypothetical facts—designed only to approximate the possible real facts. I'll read you the original paragraph again, Listen to it."

He read rapidly:

"They went down to the shore. It was high above the water. They sat down on the bank. It was a lonely spot. It was not very dark because of the reflection of the starlight from the water, Anita said: 'I do not have to marry you.' They almost quarreled. Then he kissed her. She was toying with the chain of a little pendant she wore about her neck. She said something to him. He answered loftily: 'You can't make me believe it, my child.' Later he suddenly pushed her off the bank."

The Doctor tossed aside the paper. "I read that to them twice. I distracted their minds for a time with a second—comparatively unimportant—test. Then I made them try and remember what I had read. One wrote this:

"They walked along by the shore front, where the bank was high. He kissed her. It was lonely, but not so dark because of the bright stars enlightening the water. Her fingers were wound in a small thing which was hanging about her neck. He quarreled with her. She said: 'You cannot make me marry you,' and he said: 'I do not believe that, child.' He knocked her violently off the bank and she fell into the water."

The Doctor hurried on, without comment: "And here is what the other one wrote, gentlemen:

"They walked along where it was high above water and sat down on the bench. It was a lonely spot. It was not dark under there because the moonlight was reflected from the water. Then he kissed her, and they almost quarreled. Anita said: 'I do have to marry you.' She was pulling at her locket, which was hanging around her neck. She said something else to him and he answered angrily: 'You cannot make me think it is my child.' And then he pushed her off the dock."

The Doctor's glance darted over the room. "Which is the guilty memory, gentlemen?"

"The last one!" Several of them chorused it.

"Yes! Of course. This latter one—written by Ramón Guiterrez!"

Ramón was on his feet. "That is a lie!"

"Is it?" The Doctor whirled on him. "I read you about a hundred words. I named some twelve separate facts. Julio Salta, with no guilty memory to confuse him, repeated most of them in substance. And in not a single instance did he change the sense of the original. But in your case it was not so easy. Your guilty memories mingled with the memory of what I read. Mingled into confusion.

"A very simple, almost infallible, psychological test, gentlemen. The mind cannot distinguish a true from a false memory, once they have become mingled in the subconscious mind. It is impossible. This Ramón remembered the dock, the bench, the moonlight—and he thought I had read them.

"She wore her locket that night. He forgot I named a pendant—naturally he thought I had said locket; his mind was centered on *which of the real incidents I had named*— and he confused the details. Julio couldn't remember the word pendant. He had no guilty knowledge of the locket, and so he omitted the word.

"And that moonlight! Ramón remembered a dock, evidently with a roof over it; and the moonlight came up from the water. The moonlight night was the fifth—the fifth—the night I told you gentlemen we would have to suspect Ramón most strongly."

"It is a lie, I tell you!" Ramón stood trembling, gripping the high back of his chair.

"Is it? Well, you needn't confess—we'll convict you easily enough without it. I read you—*'She said, I do not have to marry you.'* You left out only one word—but it changed the sense, completely, changed it to the real facts which your guilty memory prompted.

"Again, Julio knew nothing of the girl's unfortunate condition. I read: *'You cannot make me believe it, my child.'* Julio naturally had no difficulty in repeating the substance of that sentence correctly. But you wrote: *'You cannot make me think it is my child.'* Almost the same words, but changing the sense completely—changing it to the true fact which you knew, but Julio did not!

"You want another item of proof? The lists you and Julio made of those articles on the table over there—Julio remembered them with normal correctness. He named *'Anita's locket,'* for instance. He had always thought of it as Anita's locket, and he called it that.

"*You* named some of the articles correctly, but you omitted the locket. It had a guilty memory for you, and you were afraid to put it on the list. More than that, Jack Bruce here was watching through a slit in the curtains. You opened the locket! Your picture was there. That frightened you, too.

"You were clever enough not to remove the picture, but you smeared it with your moistened thumb—left Julio's picture, but made your own unrecognizable! An impulsive, not very sensible thing to do. But you are impulsive, aren't you? You murdered Anita on impulse—we'll admit that. Oh, so you do want to confess? Take him over there, Marberry—hear him out."

Ramón had suddenly broken. "I did not plan to do it! I did not even realize I had done it—until I saw her struggling there in the water. I was mad—insane. We had been trying to plan what we should do, but there was not anything we could do. I pushed her in! Then I was frightened—but I let her go down.

"We would have told her father. But she said he would beat her. She ran away from home so they wouldn't find it out. And she was only fifteen—they would have sent me to jail. They would never have let me marry her—and her father would have sent me to jail.

"It seemed so much easier for me—this way with her in the water—and it seemed that it might be easier for her, too. I couldn't think. I just—pushed her in and stood there watching her die. And I loved her! *Niñita, mia*—I loved her! *Ay Dios mio*—"

He broke down completely, babbling in Spanish as the detective led him aside.

The Doctor gazed after him. "The pity of it, gentlemen! Reckless, heedless, inexperience of youth, so self-confident until real trouble comes—then so helpless. Can we blame that pretty little fifteen-year-old girl? Can we blame this boy of eighteen? He's a murderer—we'll make him pay a just penalty.

"And yet—doesn't it seem, gentlemen, that we who are older could convince youth how incompetent it is to get out of trouble unaided? This Anita and Ramón—how much better a solution could have been reached for them! Yet they were afraid to tell."

The Doctor's voice turned very solemn. "This thing we have faced here tonight happens so frequently. And sometimes I wonder—just who is to blame. Respectable, hard-working families, loving parents—children who never before had caused the least trouble. Yet the girl and her unborn child are dead, and the boy is a murderer. It's rather a pity, isn't it?"

THE MIND BEYOND CONTROL

"**WE FEEL SURE** that one or other of those two young men did it"—the Doctor gazed at the group of assembled members of the Scientific Club—"but which one we—"

"What did you say their names were?" the Banker demanded.

"Roberto Lopez and Alfio Pera. Both are American born, of Sicilian parentage. The parents of the girl also are from Palermo. Three respectable, well-meaning families. But the heritage—it so frequently brings this impulsive, hot-blooded sort of crime—"

"The girl—" the Astronomer began.

"One Lucia Mendoza. A sparkling, black-eyed girl of nineteen. She was a flirt. Both Roberto and Alfio were in love with her. The motive for her murder is obvious. Jealousy—the suitor finally rejected—a sudden burst of uncontrollable frenzy. She was stabbed with a tiny silver dagger in the form of a cross. With a guard over its point, she wore it as an ornament, dangling from her neck. A family heirloom—connected, I believe, with some tradi-tional vendetta in which the Mendozas were once engaged back in Sicily."

"You mean this crime is the outcome of a vendetta?" the Banker asked.

"No, George; of course not. The girl was wearing the

ornament. The young man saw it hanging from her neck. Doubtless they were quarreling. On impulse he jerked it loose—stabbed her with it—"

"Might she not have stabbed herself with it?" the Chemist suggested. "A suicide—"

"No. She was stabbed a dozen times, after she was dead, very probably—stabbed in the side and the back. Clearly a murderous, frenzied attack. And the position of the body also—lying down there on the railroad track—"

"Suppose you give us the exact details," the Lawyer suggested.

"I will. Briefly, on the night of Aug. 25 last, in the Westchester hills, the body of Lucia Mendoza was found in a railroad cut—found about midnight by a man passing in an automobile along the adjacent roadway. The body was still warm; it was thought that the murder was committed very shortly before.

"The conformation of the country at this point has a bearing upon the case. An isolated region—a wooded locality a mile and a half from the nearest village, Appleton, where the three families in question all live. At the place where the body was found the railroad runs through a cut about twenty feet deep. There is a babbling stream in the cut, with a footpath between it and the railroad track. The body was found lying partly on the path, with an arm and shoulder over one of the rails. No train had passed during the half-hour preceding its discovery, or it would have been struck. No train was due to pass there during that half-hour—a fact which tends to prove that the murder was done between eleven-thirty and midnight.

"The man passing in the automobile was on the road,

which does not enter the railroad cut, but rises to the twenty foot higher ground beside it. The road is close to the brink of the cut. The moon had just emerged from storm-clouds which previously were threatening. The man saw the dark form of the body lying down there on the track. He investigated—and took the body on to Appleton. He is a leading citizen of Appleton; we can accept his testimony—and that of the two friends with him—as being true concerning the position of the body.

"The small dagger was in one of the wounds. The girl was dressed in a black skirt with a white blouse. Her hair was done high on her head, in Latin style, with a large shell comb in it. And over it was a long filmy black scarf—the mantilla. Those are about all the details—"

"No footprints in the path—no fingerprints on the weapon?" the Banker demanded.

"No. The dagger bore none. The ground around there is hard—marked in places with fragments of many pedestrians' prints; but none which could be identified."

"What about the testimony of the suspects, and the families?" the Bacteriologist asked.

"The girl's parents say that Lucia was a dutiful daughter. Obviously, both Roberto Lopez and Alfio Pera were in love with her. They were both eligible young men. Her parents anticipated one of them for a son-in-law. Which one the girl favored no one knew. Perhaps—until just before the tragedy—she did not know herself. On the evening of Aug. 25, her parents say, she went out surreptitiously. Or, if one of the young men called for her, her parents did not know it. When she had not returned at midnight, they were very much worried. Then came the news of the finding of her body."

"What about the young men?" the Banker suggested. "That's more important."

The Doctor nodded. "Quite so. The parents of Roberto Lopez assert that he was at home with them all that evening—that he did not go out at all. The Peras testify the same thing regarding Alfio. Both the young men maintain that they were at home—that they know nothing whatever concerning the murder."

The Doctor raised his hand to silence several questions. "I have given you our theories of what probably occurred, gentlemen. They are theories unsupported by proof. The proof, as given by the parents of the two suspects, will establish their innocence unless we can overthrow it. Both Roberto and Alfio admit they liked Lucia, and were much in her company. But that particular evening they claim they were at home."

"Perhaps it's true," commented the Lawyer.

"Perhaps. Or perhaps not. Probably not—when you come to guess at probabilities. The young men and their parents are all obviously frightened. They all act as though they were lying: the innocent family frightened at the impending danger to their son; the guilty—well, they have good cause to be frightened. Assuming one of the lads guilty—he then, of course, was not at home all that evening. He doubtless tells his parents he is innocent of the murder. But, having no alibi, it is perfectly natural that they should try to establish one for him. Fearing that he is guilty, but being unwilling to believe it—you know, gentlemen, that many loving parents would lie stoutly to save their son."

"Did the girl have no other admirers?" the Astronomer asked.

"No. It seems not. In any event, if anyone other than these two murdered her, the case may never be solved. We must ignore that possibility. These two are the most likely suspects—and with them the police agree that we of the Scientific Club may be able to help. The tangible evidence against them is insufficient for an arrest, much less a conviction. Detective Marberry—"

The door opened; an attendant announced: "They're here. Dr. Adams."

"Bring them up," commanded the Doctor. He added briskly: "Our assumption, gentlemen, is merely that one of these two suspects, in all probability, is guilty. Discarding all motive—all legal evidence—we have the condition that *if* one of them is guilty, the guilty knowledge of his crime is in his mind. Our purpose is to dig out that guilty knowledge—lay it bare—and thus convict him. Detective Marberry is here with the young men. If neither has any guilty knowledge, we will fail, of course. But no harm will be done."

The Doctor gestured toward the quiet, grave-faced Alienist who sat beside him. "Dr. Gregg here believes that, under these present conditions, the guilty mind will be unable to withhold its guilt." He nodded toward the Photographer. "Mr. Malden, in his studio, has prepared for us a series of—"

Again the door opened; Detective Marberry entered with the two suspects. Roberto Lopez, the older by a year, was tall, heavy-set for a Latin. Yet not stout; stalwart and muscular. A handsome young man, with sleek black hair, dark eyes with heavy black brows, and a dark, ruddy complexion. He was dressed in a neat business suit, and wore a straw hat.

Alfio Pera was of the dapper type. Small and slender, with pointed tan shoes, white linen trousers pressed to a razor edge, and a blue serge coat pinched at the waist. A gray felt slouch hat with a vivid band. A youth of rakish, debonair personality. A handsome face, though rather pale, inclining to sallowness; dark eyes, black hair, and a very small black moustache.

Both the newcomers smiled with an effort to be ingratiating as the Doctor briefly introduced them. They took the chairs he indicated, a few feet apart from one another, at a side of the room facing most of the club members. The Doctor turned his chair to confront them; the detective unobtrusively slipped to one side, standing back against the wall where they did not notice him, but where he could observe them closely.

Under the curious scrutiny of the onlookers, it was obvious that both were uneasy and frightened, though making an effort not to appear so. Outwardly they desired to do what they were told. Roberto stated it at once, and Alfio asked why they had been summoned—what they were to do.

Beneath their ingratiating manner toward the Doctor, it was apparent also that an animosity was between them. They avoided each other—had not spoken one to the other since first they entered the clubroom; and the glances they occasionally exchanged were full of hatred. Perhaps the guilty one feared the other's impending accusation? Or the innocent one suspected, or knew, of his companion's guilt? Was one of them indeed guilty? Could his mind withhold that guilt? Or would the Doctor and the Alienist draw it from him against his will? The questions were forcing themselves upon the club members. Several of the men were whispering together until the Doctor sharply silenced them. A look that the dapper Alfio cast at his stalwart companion made the Doctor say abruptly:

"You two have told the police that you know nothing whatever of this murder. I'm wondering whether that is not a lie. You, Alfio—you think Roberto did it, don't you?"

Alfio was seated low in a big leather chair, his felt hat on his knee, a cigarette between his thin fingers. He looked up to meet the Doctor's gaze.

"Why, yes, that is what I think," he answered slowly. "But—"

"He lies!" Roberto declared angrily. His dark face was flushed. "I have thought all this time he was saying that to the police: that is a lie—he did it himself—"

"How do you know?" demanded the Doctor.

"I do not. I know nothing about it. I was at home that night."

The Doctor turned back to Alfio. "You think Roberto did it? Why?"

Again Alfio waited an instant before replying slowly: "I was saying to you I think he did it, but I do not know. I was at home—"

The Doctor interrupted. "Yes, we realize that. I'll ask you both this: Which one of you was Lucia in love with?"

"With me," they both answered simultaneously.

The Doctor laughed ironically. "You were both sure of her love, weren't you? Didn't she throw one of you over for the other? We believe she did, and we want to find out which one."

They did not answer that. Out of the silence, Alfio said: "What is it you want of me here, Dr. Adams?"

The Doctor's grim tone belied his smile as he answered: "We're not satisfied that you are both innocent. But if you are, we're going to give you a chance to prove it. You want that, don't you?"

Roberto nodded vehemently. Alfio said:

"My innocence is proven. They—my father and mother—have told you—"

"One moment," the Doctor broke in sternly. "We're not here to argue. Nor am I going to explain anything in detail. Either you'll do what I tell you—or you refuse. Which is it?" He eyed them. "If one of you refuses, we'll know he is guilty—afraid of our test. And we'll convict him by some method—you may be sure of that. Which one of you refuses?"

Roberto smiled. "I am willing to do what you want, Dr. Adams."

Alfio said: "I have not anything to be afraid of. What is it that you want me to do?" And he also smiled.

But neither smile was convincing, and the suppressed apprehension of them both was more apparent than ever.

The Doctor relaxed. "Thank you. That will help us a good deal. I'll tell you what you are to do—the purpose of it need not concern you. First, I want you to listen closely while I tell these gentlemen how Lucia was murdered."

He turned to the club members. "I find it necessary to

repeat the salient points, gentlemen. This railroad cut is about twenty feet deep, with a footpath and stream down there beside the track. It is a secluded spot—you can barely see the path from the road above. Lucia and—one of these young men—were walking along and quarreling. On impulse he stabbed her. She lay dead, partly on the path, with an arm over one of the rails. He gazed down at her, confused and terrified at what he had done." The Doctor repeated, slowly and with emphasis: "For quite a while he stood there, gazing down at that silent form of his victim; then he turned and ran away.... That's all, gentlemen.... Mr. Malden, let me have those photographs, please."

Both the suspects started. The Doctor added smilingly: "You have nothing to fear—no, of course, we weren't able to take photographs of the actual murder."

The Photographer produced two stacks of small photographs mounted on cards about six inches square. There seemed some fifty cards in each bundle, held by a rubber band. The Doctor drew his chair up to a table which had on it an electrolier. Simultaneously, the Very Young Man switched off the room's other lights. Shadows sprang up. The table was bathed in a yellow glow, with a circle of light on the floor about it. Everywhere else was gloom, with the silent, listening club members enshrouded.

The Doctor placed the two bundles of photographs on the table. The Alienist sat quietly beside him, a trifle withdrawn, so that he was just outside the circle of light; the detective had advanced, but he kept within the shadow.

The Doctor slipped the bands from the bundles of photographs. "Come here, please, you two. Bring those small chairs—sit here across the table from me."

They took the positions he indicated. The table electrolier shone full upon them as they sat down. They were
facing the secluded Alienist and the detective across the
table.

The Doctor said quietly: "Mr. Malden made this series
of photographs in his studio. There are two identical sets
of them—four dozen separate pictures in each set.... Here,
look at one."

He handed the top card of each stack across the table.
The fingers that took them were trembling visibly as Alfio
and Roberto bent over to examine the picture. A scene
quite dark—almost a silhouette: a vague outline of steel
rail, with the huddled form of a woman lying there. The
tones of the picture were black ranging to gray. Nothing else. And only the general outlines of the figure were
distinguishable—very few of the details.

The Doctor went on: "Mr. Malden used three models—a
girl and two young men. You will easily distinguish
between the men. One is large, with a straw hat. That
represents you, Roberto. The other is more slender, with a
soft slouch hat, to represent Alfio. Those are the types of
hat you each habitually wear, we understand. We used them
in the pictures because the outlines of them can be seen so
readily.... Here, glance at some of the others."

He gave them each a complete bundle. The room was
dead silent, save for the slight scuffling of the cards as they
looked at them. In each picture either the girl was lying
there alone or one or other of the men was bending over
her.

The Doctor continued slowly: "I want you to look over
these pictures very carefully. Divide your set into two

piles—the pictures you think represent the scene of the murder, and those which do not. Imagine yourself an eye-witness. Select the pictures which show the scene as it would have looked to you, the eye-witness. Pictures of the girl as she must have looked lying there alone—also as she must have looked with the murderer with her. If you want to establish your complete innocence, now is your chance—"

"But—" interrupted Roberto apprehensively.

"What?"

"How can I do that? I do not know anything about the murder."

"No. I appreciate that. But you know you weren't there, and some of the pictures show that you were. And you've heard how Lucia was found lying with an arm and shoulder over the railroad rail. Discard all the pictures you please—keep only those which you conceive to represent the real scene. Do it carefully. Some of them do not even look like Lucia. Mr. Malden used a second woman for some of them—an older, stouter woman. We'll know you are trying to fool us if you select one of those. Just pick out the correct scenes as they would have looked had you been there as an eye-witness."

Alfio made an effort to smile. "My opinion will be worth nothing to you, Dr. Adams. But if you think it will be—I believe I can select—though I am not sure, of course—"

"You can," said the Doctor. "Take plenty of time."

They were both intelligent youths. The Doctor's reasons for the test, as he gave them, were thinly veiled and unconvincing. Obviously, neither believed him. If guilty, one of them undoubtedly realized he was being forced into a trap.

But, without betraying himself, there was nothing he could do. He went into it, alarmed, but wary—confident, probably, that he could avoid it.

In silence they pored over the cards, selecting, sorting, considering long and carefully on some, on others deciding almost at a glance. Frequently, each gave a sidelong look at what the other was doing. A tenseness had fallen upon the room, broken by the shuffling of feet and occasional whispers from the watching scientists in the shadows. The Doctor sat impassive; the detective and the Alienist had moved closer to the table, gazing keenly into the faces of the two young men.

At length the selections were made. Roberto had picked about twenty-five scenes to represent the murder; and Alfio about twenty. The Doctor took the two piles. Alfio said: "You will see that I—"

"Wait, please." With the Alienist at his elbow, they examined the selected pictures. Roberto began: "I do not understand how—"

But the Doctor shut him up.

Another interval passed. Frequently the Alienist and the Doctor whispered together; the pictures were spread out before them in rows under the light. Then the Alienist said aloud: "It's obvious, Adams."

The words caused a stir in the room.

"Quiet!" The Doctor was on his feet, standing now in the shadow. The Alienist was still poring over the cards. The detective had slipped around the table and was standing now close behind the chairs of Roberto and Alfio.

From the semi-darkness came the Doctor's voice: "The first thing these young men did, gentlemen, was just what you would expect them to do. Ten of the pictures showed a man's figure with a straw hat, and ten a man with a felt hat. Roberto discarded all those with the straw hat, and retained all those with the felt hat. And Alfio did exactly the reverse. That was natural—each to protect himself and accuse the other. These pictures were selected swiftly, without thought of other details. For instance, Alfio included two straw-hat scenes where the girl's figure was obviously too stout to represent Lucia. Roberto did the same. Yet they both knew better, for both of them discarded all the other scenes in which the stout figure was shown.

"So much for that. In the majority of cases, however, the girl is shown alone. To these they gave more consideration." The Doctor's voice rose to sudden grimness. "We have here a group of pictures made by a mind which obviously is innocent—and a mind which obviously is guilty!... Be quiet, you two! We don't want any more evidence from either of you!... In selecting these latter scenes, gentlemen, the innocent and the guilty mind were working from totally different angles. The innocent mind had a mental picture of the scene based on what he *imagined* Lucia looked like as she lay there murdered—what he had been told by the police and by me of the crime. But the guilty mind had more than that—had a knowledge of the actual event as he remembered it. Which, subconsciously but inevitably, influenced his selection.

"For instance, some of the pictures show the mantilla with the high comb under it; and some show the mantilla without the high bulge of the comb. The innocent mind never thought of this detail and instinctively included both. He had never heard exactly how Lucia was dressed that fatal evening. His imagination subconsciously depicted her as he remembered her in life—sometimes with the comb and sometimes without it."

"But the guilty mind selected all the pictures *without* the comb—and discarded all in which the comb was evident. He was on his guard, this murderer. He had never been told that Lucia wore the comb that night—he did not have to be told, for he *knew* it, remembered it! He was on his guard—and just clever enough to think that he could avoid the trap by keeping away from the pictures which show that true detail.

"Possibly all a coincidence, gentlemen? Oh, yes; almost anything is *possible*. But there was something about those pictures which this murderer did not notice at all—and the guilty knowledge in his mind came out! You remember, gentlemen, the whole assumption of this case has been that the murderer walked with the girl along that footpath by the track. The innocent mind assumed that—but it wasn't the fact. The murderer and the girl came along the upper road, at the edge of the embankment, twenty feet above the path and the track. We know it, because the body was broken by the fall. He killed her up there at the roadside, dragged her body to the edge, and tumbled it down. We could not identify any footprints, but in the gravel up there the dragging of the body showed."

At a signal from the Doctor, the Very Young Man switched on the room's main lights. The Doctor exclaimed: "The guilty pictures were selected by you, Roberto Lopez! Yours is the guilty mind—"

The detective leaped forward. "*You* killed her! You needn't deny it—we've got you—"

Roberto was on his feet, struggling to free himself from the detective's grasp. Alfio sat back, his face pale but flooded with relief. Roberto protested: "Let me go! That's a lie! I was at home, I tell you. I don't know a thing about it—I chose those pictures because you told me I must. But I don't know anything—"

"Oh, you don't?" The Doctor's voice was caustic. "You needn't confess—we won't need your confession. Your own mind—beyond your control—has betrayed you. We had no choice between you and Alfio—absolutely none. A while ago, I implanted in your minds the words: '*This murderer stood there looking down at the silent form of his victim.*' To Alfio, that meant standing beside the body, looking down at it. His imagination instinctively worked that way, because he was innocent. But your guilty mind made you unconsciously interpret those words differently. You had a mental picture of that body as it looked from the top of that twenty-foot embankment. There is where you stood looking down at it."

"I did not! I didn't do it, I tell you!"

"You lie! You've betrayed yourself! Your conscious mind was occupied with eliminating those straw-hat scenes, and with avoiding that high, protruding shell-comb under the mantilla.... Ah! You realize now how true that is! Well, that kept your mind busy; but your subconscious mind was free, and all the while it was working against you. Here's something about those pictures you didn't notice!

"Half of them—and only half—were taken from the ground level. For the other half, Mr. Malden had his camera eight or ten feet above the figures, looking down at them from an angle. It gave them quite a different perspective. Not enough to be noticeable as such—but enough so that Alfio, conceiving everything from the ground level, instinctively did not pick them. But to *your* guilty mind, these were the ones which looked more natural. You were trying to imagine yourself an eye-witness, but your imagination was distorted by your guilt. It never occurred to you to imagine how the scene would look from down in the cut, for the memory of the body as you saw it from above was too strong within you. And so you chose the pictures of that slanting perspective without realizing why!"

The detective was insisting: "You killed her! Planned it deliberately—"

"No! No, I did not! I mean—yes, I killed her, but I did not plan it! She would not marry me—she said she would marry Alfio if he asked her. I stabbed her like you say—we were up there on the road, yes; but I did not plan—"

The detective led him aside. The Doctor added—

"I think that's all, gentlemen. It's difficult—almost impossible—to control the workings of one's guilty mind when it is being probed in such a way as this."

ASHES OF GUILT

1

THE CHEMIST SMILED grimly. "True enough. Five logical suspects, gentlemen. One simple, commonplace motive—the old man's money. Except the housemaid. She was not an heir."

"Wait," exclaimed the Banker. "Don't dash into it this way. *I* don't know anything about it yet." He gazed at the group of scientists assembled in the small private clubroom. "Who got murdered? Won't somebody tell me?"

"I'll explain it all, George," said the Chemist quietly. "It was old man Grayley—you've met him, haven't you?"

"Grayley? Member of the club?"

"Yes. Harrison J. Grayley."

"Oh." The Banker sat back. "Yes. Think I did once. Long time ago—a fat man—he ate too much."

"A scientist," said the Chemist unsmilingly, "whose work in bacteriology has been invaluable. That was years ago." He addressed the room in general. "A good many of you will need the details of the case. Harrison Grayley was murdered about two weeks past. A man of sixty-eight—retired from work for some years. He lived in Allison Hills. Seldom came to the city—has not been in the club for two years."

The Astronomer said: "I knew him, Rogers. Quaint old fellow. To think—murdered—"

"Wealthy," commented the Inventor, to no one in particular.

"He deserved it," put in the Surgeon. "His research work in—"

"Don't let's argue his research work," expostulated the Banker impatiently. "I came here because Rogers said he had a murder case. All I've heard is five suspects—"

"An unfortunate case for the police," the Chemist resumed. "Five suspects, and they cannot make an arrest. The evidence—rather queer evidence, by the way—applies equally to—"

"You'd better give George the main details first," the Doctor warned.

"I will," nodded the Chemist. "The case, gentlemen, may possibly be decided here tonight. They're coming here— I've sent for them." He glanced at his watch. "True enough. I must be brief. In a word—for those of you who did not know him—Harrison Grayley was a man about average height, but exceedingly stout. A gourmand—he loved his food above everything.

"For all that, he was in good health—suffering only from gout. This, though it could not check his eating, he did suffer from severely. Almost continuously house-ridden, nursing a foot which would not bear his weight.

"Yet, gentlemen, a likable character—mighty likable. But dogmatic, gruff. Strike him right; have him like you; he'd entertain you in princely fashion. But cross him—get him down on you—" The Chemist shrugged expressively. "I'd hate to have to live with him then."

"Has this got anything to do with his murder?" demanded the Banker. "We know all that—"

The detective was on him like a hawk, twisting him around.

"It has, of course. One of the suspects is the family *chef,* an heir and exceedingly important member of Grayley's household, in his service many years. So much for that. And as for Grayley's bad temper, if he gets down on you— well, gentlemen, he's been at odds continuously with every member of his family.

"The murder was discovered by Elsie Queal, English housemaid. She went into his room to build a fire in his grate—the house was run Continental style—went into his room one morning, to find him dead in bed. A knife buried to the hilt in his back. This maid—we consider her one of the suspects, yet she is the only one who seems to have had no motive. She had been there but a few months. A suspect only because she was in the house. It had not been broken into; the murder obviously was what the police call an inside job.

"The knife, with no fingerprints on it, none to be found anywhere, in fact, was identified as belonging to the kitchen equipment. Anyone of the family could have used it, of course. The housemaid—possibly to lead suspicion to the *chef.* He is Pierre Vanchi, an artist in his line, according to his employer. His motive would be the fact that he was an heir to the sum of fifteen thousand dollars, and he knew it. So far as can be determined now, he drew a good salary, was contented and had a real affection for Grayley, which the old man returned.

"There was in the house that night no one else save the three members of Grayley's family. An unusual family. Grayley never married. Thirty-eight years ago, a man of thirty, and then a rising young scientist, he had an unfortunate love affair. The girl died. Deciding never to marry, he adopted a child, an orphan girl of two years named Alice.

"Brought her up, loved her devotedly. But of late years he has grown to dislike her. She came of criminal parents— one of them dying in jail. She caused Grayley considerable unhappiness. Eloped at seventeen with one Heinrich Bundt, rather a worthless character. They have one son. Later Grayley became reconciled to Alice, wanted her back with him. She came, and brought her family with her. Grayley has had them with him for the last five years. Made them his heirs.

"A worthless man, this Bundt. And his son is as bad, a wild, reckless sort of youth, now twenty-two. The woman— she is forty now—living on the old man's money, putting on society airs—all three of them quarreling with him constantly. Yet he stood it, because doubtless in his heart he still loved the Alice he had adopted years ago."

The Chemist paused slightly, then added: "One of these five is probably the criminal, gentlemen. The specific evidence at the scene of the crime is peculiarly unfortunate. We believe that someone of these five, with or without the knowledge of some of the others, entered Grayley's room that night—he seldom locked his door—and stabbed him as he slept.

"His room is remote from the rest of the household; any slight noise would not have aroused the house. And he was a heavy sleeper, easy enough to stab him as he slept.

"The evidence is unfortunate because, though it indicates the criminal, it gives a choice. All have been questioned and accused, but to no purpose. They protest innocence. The specific evidence has been kept from them. I doubt if any of them know the startling clues we have—evidence kept from them, because it could never convict, and if used by police routine, it might only serve to put them further on their guard. They are all very wary now, expecting an arrest—"

"What is the evidence?" demanded the Banker.

The Chemist turned to the Very Young Man. "Jack, bring that in, will you? I'll show it now, and then—"

As the Very Young Man rose, the Chemist added sharply: "Wait, Jack!"

The door was opening. "Mr. Bundt and family to see you, Mr. Rogers."

"Bring them in." As the attendant withdrew, the Chemist said hastily: "No more now, gentlemen. I believe I can fasten the crime on one of them. This evidence—you'll see—"

"Do *we* have anything to do?" asked the Banker anxiously.

"No. Just sit quiet. An audience—so that I can explain about the evidence—make them think— Sh! Here they are."

2

THE ATTENDANT USHERED five of them into the room. Amid a confusion of introductions they took their seats, the three Bundts in a group a trifle apart from the club members, the two servants near and slightly behind them. Interesting individuals; the scientists regarded them curiously. The Bundts bore themselves with an air of repressed defiance.

The woman was modishly, expensively gowned. A tall, powerful-looking woman, with black hair and dark eyes set too close together. A face almost beautiful, yet unpleasant. Perhaps it was her expression of the moment, a haughty, superior air of resentment that one of her station should be annoyed in this fashion. Or perhaps it was something deeper, her innate character.

Her husband, known to the family as Heinie, was a man just under fifty. A rotund, flabby figure, but with powerful, heavy shoulders. A red face of sagging jowls, pale watery eyes and a slack mouth. A face which in alcoholic circumstances might be jolly, but which now was sullen with a dumb aspect of alarm. A well-dressed man, with expensive jewelry, none of which could hide the fact that he had never done anything worthwhile in life—and never would.

To this latter extent Heinie's son George resembled him. A husky, well-built lad of twenty-two, jauntily dressed, with the supercilious air of his mother, which in him was merely insolence.

The maid, Elsie Queal, was of the self-effacing type which ordinarily would draw little attention. A woman in her twenties, rather plain of feature—a woman as low-class English as Heinie evidently was German. She sat stiff and straight in her chair, quite obviously conscious of herself and her best clothes she was wearing; her manner partly fear, partly the aspect of one who resents being insulted.

Of them all, only one seemed of likable personality. Pierre Vanchi, the chef. A big, round, jellylike figure—bald head, with a moon face beneath it, and an absurdly small black mustache.

In his kitchen, white-aproned and white-capped, Pierre would doubtless have been a commanding figure, smiling and jolly, yet stern that everything should be of perfect creation. Now, however, with his tight collar and pinched-back coat of French model, gray-striped trousers stuffed with the fullness of his fat legs, and very shiny pointed shoes—he seemed thoroughly ill at ease.

And alarmed as well, with an air of anxiety to please, to placate everybody. He bowed elaborately to the club members, eyed the Chemist, and smiled weakly; and then sat awkwardly on the chair given him, with his gray felt hat on his knees.

Such were the five members of Harrison Grayley's household, one of whom the Chemist had declared probably murdered him.

As the room quieted, the Chemist said: "I have asked you visitors here for what we may call an informal inquiry into the death of Mr. Grayley.... Just a moment please—"

Mrs. Bundt was about to interrupt him. As he checked her, she sat back, angrily fingering her necklace; and her husband said in an undertone: "Take it easy, Alice."

"An informal inquiry," the Chemist went on. "As I promised you when you agreed to come, it will not last long, and it will do much to free you from further annoyance from the police."

"That's what we want," said Heinie Bundt. "These crazy police—"

"Yes, I understand how you feel. I told you our inquiry here may clear up several things which must be disposed of before the matter can be dropped—"

"We don't care whether it's dropped or not," declared young George Bundt. "All we want is to be let alone, because we're not guilty and we're damned sick of—"

"George!" Heinie waved his son down with a vehement gesture; but the mother nodded her equally vehement approval. It was evident that mother and son were blusteringly aggressive; but Heinie, like Pierre, was anxious to placate.

"Quite so," smiled the Chemist imperturbably. "Well, I hope that tonight will settle it one way or the other— Ah, Marberry! Hello, Sergeant Croft. I've been waiting for you, stalling along hoping you'd arrive."

The door had opened unceremoniously to admit four men, two policemen in uniform and two detectives. The Bundts—father and son—were on their feet; the color drained from Mrs. Bundt's face, leaving a splotch of red rouge on each cheek; the two servants shrank in their chairs with gasps of alarm.

"Sit down!" commanded the Chemist. "If I got you—any

of you visitors—here under false pretense, I can only claim that it was necessary. Sit down, Sergeant. You. Marberry—here, sit by me." He whispered to the detective aside: "Just started on them. We're all ready; I'll hammer 'em now. Watch closely; give me any pointers you can."

Aloud, he resumed: "No cause for any of you to be perturbed, if you are innocent." The Bundts sat down.

"Thanks. That's better. I'm going to question you. Will you all answer me freely? Or do you want to make trouble? We can arrest you, if we wish. I imagine you know the law isn't afraid of your money."

"I'll answer your questions," declared Mrs. Bundt. "But I've already been insulted enough. I should think—"

The Chemist waved away her statement. "To be wholly frank, I'll say that we are convinced now that one of you five murdered Harrison Grayley."

They were prepared for it. There was no outburst; only Pierre who mumbled: *"Non! Non!"* and waved his pudgy hands in horror. The others—as though with the realization that this was more serious than anything which had gone before—sat firm.

"One of you is the criminal," the Chemist persisted. "I'm going to give you straight talk; this won't take long, as I promised, because I'm going to the root of it at once. Sergeant Croft here, of Allison Hills, very shortly discovered far more of the circumstances of the murder than was ever revealed to you. Ah, that surprises you, doesn't it? Well, it's true.

"There were reasons—technical, legal reasons, if you please, which you do not understand and which do not concern you—why he thought it better not to make an arrest at once. Yet, almost from the first, he has known, has had the proof of who killed Harrison Grayley!"

It was a bombshell which threw consternation into the visitors. Detective Marberry whispered to the Chemist: "Struck at them all! But still, I'm sure—"

"Yes. Watch closely." Aloud, the Chemist added grimly: "I'm speaking now only to the one who is guilty." His gaze passed from one to the other, rested on each accusingly; and each in turn flinched under it.

Pierre tried to smile. *"Mon Dieu!* You make me feel I am a murderer! But I loved him! For so many years I have—"

George Bundt protested: "Trying to frighten us! Let him try, mother; much good it'll do him."

The woman sneered. Only Heinie Bundt and the maid said nothing. Heinie gripped the arms of his chair, his face fallen into sullen stupidity, masking, perhaps nothing, perhaps everything. And the maid, seeming ready to burst forth into voluble protestations, but thinking better of it and remaining silent.

3

"**WE KNOW WHO** is guilty," the Chemist repeated. He turned away from the suspects to the room in general; but the detective continued to watch keenly their every move, every expression.

"A queer case, gentlemen," said the Chemist. "Sergeant Croft had, almost at once, evidence of the identity of the criminal. He chose to make the arrest before you, here tonight—a question of legal expediency involving the immunity a possible confession might give.

"You do not understand me—these visitors do not understand—and it is not necessary that any of you should. Enough to say that Marberry and Sergeant Croft preferred me to handle the case here before you. We are about to make an arrest.

"Sit down, George Bundt! If you annoy me further, we'll arrest *you*, innocent or guilty! I have you all here now—all five of you—got you here under false pretenses, if you like. But you're here, and you'll listen to me quietly whether you want to or not!"

The Chemist's voice grew less vehement.

"Gentlemen, I'm going to detail the events of the murder for you. Elsie Queal, here—" The maid started at this abrupt mention of her name— "discovered the body of

Grayley. A kitchen knife was buried in his back. Evidently he had been murdered in his sleep; had never awakened.

"But, gentlemen, here is the part we have not so far disclosed. He did awaken. He was stabbed while asleep in bed, no doubt. Left there for dead. But he did not stay there. In a death agony, yet with all his faculties, he crawled from bed. The knife was still in him. He reached for it. Could not pluck it out. Crawled then from bed to his small desk across the room. It was a moonlight night; the room probably was moonlit. Yet he lighted the electrolier fastened to his desk, and died there in the desk chair."

As though fascinated, the visitors sat listening to the Chemist's words. Forgetful of themselves now, forgetful of the detective's watchful eyes.

"How do we know all this? Simply enough. The wound was in Grayley's back. With the knife in it, there probably was at first no great flux of blood. Yet enough to wet his fingers as he groped around spasmodically to reach it. With the knife in that position he could not get it out. But blood stained his fingers. The cord of the desk electrolier had blood on it, and there were blood smudges on the large desk blotter, mingled with the ink spots which had been there before.

"The murdered man's blood, gentlemen. You may say, how do we know that? Might not the criminal have had blood-stained fingers as well? To that we say, no. This criminal left no fingerprints on the weapon. A swiftly executed deed, but evidently done with some forethought. To deliver a blow like that—to leave the knife in his body and escape from the room at once, gave no cause for having blood-stained fingers. And we have, too, another reason for knowing all this—which I'll give you in a moment.

"Let me reconstruct the crime in still more detail. Someone crept through that dark, silent house, went to the pantry, secured the knife, went to Mr. Grayley's bedroom, stabbed him. And stood there in the moonlight watching his death struggles as he died. We know that, because we know that Grayley did not die at once; and the criminal must have lingered there, because we know that Grayley was aware of who had struck the blow!

"Then Grayley lost consciousness, ceased his struggles and was left for dead. And it was after that—a moment, or longer we do not know—that Grayley must have recovered consciousness, still with strength left to drag himself from his bed. The criminal with the deed done, nevertheless, was torn by fear, with thoughts that perhaps something might have gone wrong in the haste of the moment.

"And so this criminal returned later to the scene of the crime and, horrified, found Grayley, not in bed, but dead in his desk chair. In a panic the body was dragged back, put into the bed. Blood was on the desk chair. With a bottom corner of a sheet, the criminal frantically wiped it away. We found smears on the bottom of the sheet which later was spread over the body.

"This terrified criminal forgot that the wound would not stain the sheet down there. And the smears on the chair were not wholly cleaned. It was all done so hastily, in terror and confusion. Other blood smears were left, and those splotches on the electrolier cord were overlooked. And blood marks on the blotter, left there in plain sight. And an ink-stained pen on the desk; the pen had blood on it, too!"

The detective whispered: "That struck home! We're right! Hurry, Rogers!"

The Chemist nodded. The room was silent, electrical, as he paused. The listening men sat tense; the five suspects did not move in their chairs, their fascinated gazes clinging to the Chemist's face. At a swift gesture from the Chemist, the Very Young Man abruptly rose to his feet.

Without warning or explanation he switched off the room's lights. Blackness for a moment. A gasp. The shuffling of feet; a stifled oath of surprise from one of the policemen loitering by the door; and in the center of the room, the sound of the Very Young Man moving something. Then a light sprang on, a narrow, white beam from up near the ceiling.

It descended vertically, leaving the room in shadow, but striking full on a small table. And on the table lay a black cloth some two feet square, a cloth bulging upward a foot from something concealed under it. In the intensely bright beam it lay, mysterious and sinister, and every eye in the room was riveted upon it. Shadows enveloped the suspects—a darkness carefully calculated to give the guilty one a sense of security from observation.

But it was a false security. A pale, unobtrusive yellow glow from a hidden light illumined their features, unnoticed by them in the clamor of attention the white beam drew; but it was enough for the detective's keen, watchful eyes. And on four of the faces he saw surprise, perturbation and curiosity; and on the other—stark terror.

The Chemist's voice rang through the silent room— swift, grim words:

"Grayley knew who had killed him, gentlemen! And as

he dragged himself there to his desk, his only purpose was to write an accusation before he died. To tell us who had killed him so that justice might be done. This murderer— Oh, yes, it was a man, we can exonerate these two women— neither would have attempted to lift Grayley's huge bulk from the floor to the bed—this murderer came back to the scene of his crime and found that his victim had written a death accusation.

"Just three words! But enough to tell us all we wanted to know! This murderer saw the words lying there—scrawled with pen and ink—and the blood-stained pen lying beside it, dropped from the man's dead fingers.

"Panic descended upon this criminal. He gazed at the three words—one of them his Christian name—damning him. Grayley in his death agony could not find note-paper. A magazine was lying on the desk. He tore from it one of its advertising pages, scrawled his three words on the white margin.

"The murderer saw all this, in a panic of terror. Then his head cleared. He snatched up the paper with its damning words, lighted a corner of it with trembling fingers, dropped it in the empty grate where it was entirely consumed. Burned it, gentlemen—destroyed this evidence against him. And when it was destroyed there before his eyes, relief flooded over him. His head was still whirling; he couldn't think clearly, couldn't reason, couldn't notice details.

"But he told himself he was safe. He put the body back in bed. No real reason why he should have bothered. But his original plan was that Grayley should die in bed. The mind under terrible stress clings dumbly to its ideas. The body, being out of bed—Grayley writing a death-note—was unexpected, dangerous. So he put the body back.

"Then he tried—hurriedly, because he was afraid to stay in the room too long—tried to wipe away the blood stains about the desk and desk chair. He evidently did wipe away most of them. But curiously enough, those most prominent—those mingled with the ink stains on blotter and pen—those he did not see. Let that pass for a moment. We know why he did not see them."

4

THE CHEMIST'S VEHEMENT words flowed on uninterrupted. "Destroyed the evidence, gentlemen! Burned it to ashes—his name written out by his victim. But did he destroy it? Look there!"

Abruptly the Very Young Man snatched away the cloth. A small glass dome was revealed. Beneath it, lying on white velvet, a crinkled, yet almost flat oblong of ashes, a burned magazine page. Fragile—too fragile to bear its own weight if lifted—yet still intact. Burned evidence! But not destroyed. For etched in the gray-black ashes, the print of the page showed clear and legible. And scrawled beside it—handwriting. Legible in the brilliant white light, clear and sharp as an etching.

"Look at it, gentlemen! Come up here, all of you. Come up and look—the murderer's name, written by his victim!"

The room was in confusion. Several of the men started to their feet.

"I—I didn't realize—" Heinie Bundt's involuntary mumble. He was standing by his chair, swaying, staring across to where under the white light, lay the damning evidence.

"Didn't realize! Of course, you didn't!" The detective like a hawk was on him, twisting him around, gripping him from behind. "Didn't realize we had you all the time, did you? Here he is, Sergeant Croft."

"I—let go of me! I didn't—" Bundt tried to jerk himself loose. "Let go of me! I didn't—I mean I didn't know writing would show on ashes—I mean—that's queer, isn't it?"

He was struggling to recover himself. Sergeant Croft was with Marberry, both of them clutching the man roughly, shoving him back against the wall. The policemen hurrying toward them.

"Trying to bluster it through, are you? With your name lying right there! *'Heinie killed me.'* You remember how it looked, don't you?"

"I—no, I never—"

"*'Heinie killed me.'* That's what he wrote, and you burned it in the grate! You think you can stand up against the fact that although you burned it, you didn't destroy it? Go look at it! Why, from here, you can read it!"

"No! He—maybe he thought I killed him—"

"And you didn't notice the blood on the pen, did you? Or on the blotter? Because, in that artificial light, you thought those spots were ink. You tried to be a railroad man when you were young. We've looked up your record; you were barred because you were color-blind! You are, aren't you?"

"No! Yes—I—yes, I am. But—"

"That's enough! We've got you! Got you every way."

Abruptly Bundt sagged to a chair.

"Yes—you—I did it! What's the good of saying I didn't, when you've got my name there? I thought—I never realized I hadn't destroyed it."

With Bundt led aside, and the two detectives questioning him, the room was restored to order. The Chemist said: "As I told you, gentlemen, the evidence was peculiarly unfortunate. We really thought from the first that Heinie Bundt was the murderer. Leaving blood stains amid the ink, but wiping away all others, suggested color blindness.

"But a point like that is wholly inconclusive. Nor did we think a woman had done it. But of that we could not be sure, until near the last, when on Bundt's face, in what he thought was darkness, we saw the guilt. But that, too, was far from proof, or a confession.

"We had the burned magazine page. There it is. The writing is legible. I won't bother you with the chemistry of combustion—enough to say that the mineral constituents of ink will not burn, and that they remain etched in the ashes of paper. The thing is obvious; there it lies, for you all to read. But look at it closely. Different kinds of paper burn differently, as well as with a different color ash.

"This one, a rather cheap magazine paper, burned flat and almost unbroken. But as you see, one end is crinkled and twisted—shriveled in the burning. You cannot straighten out that shriveled portion; it would fall into fragments if you touched it. The writing there is irrevocably gone—destroyed forever.

"Peculiarly unfortunate as legal proof, for if you look closely, you'll see the ashes read: '——e killed me.' Quite obviously the Christian name of the criminal, but that name is all missing save the last letter. The whole thing in handwriting easily recognized as that of Grayley's.

"But whose Christian name? Grayley would instinctively call every member of his household by the first name. But which name was it? Heinie, or Alice, or George, Pierre or Elsie? The letter 'e' is a very common ending for given names. But unfortunate that all in this family should have it.

"So this proof, legally used, meant nothing. We have had, therefore, to build carefully into Heinie's mind the conviction that he was irrevocably trapped. He saw the evidence there under the dome—from a distance of ten feet.

"He could see the handwriting—and I told him what the three words were—after he had exposed his guilt to us. Told him his name was there and, of course, he assumed it was—remembered exactly how it had looked before he burned it."

The Chemist smiled at the club members. "I think that's all, gentlemen. Jack, will you remove the evidence? Careful! It's very fragile."

THE ENCYCLOPEDIC SLEUTH

1

"**HER NAME WAS** Anna Crane," said the Chemist. "She died—murder, suicide, accident, as you like—died of hydrocyanic acid poisoning."

"What's that?" demanded the Banker. "Never heard of it."

"Oh, yes, you have, George. Prussic acid—you've heard of that, haven't you? Gentlemen, this promised to be a most unfortunate case for Mr. Blaine—" The Chemist turned smilingly to the man beside him, and then again addressed the group of scientists assembled in the clubroom.

"Mr. Blaine is assistant district attorney of Prince County—Milton, Long Island, you know. The death occurred there—in the south shore village of Cliffside—"

The Astronomer said: "It was murder, wasn't it, Rogers?"

"We think so—yes. But the superficial evidence was conclusive of nothing. Beneath those superficial circumstances—well, Mr. Blaine was discussing them with me, and I suggested Detective Marberry. We found very speedily that it was a case which, if it could be brought to a successful conclusion at all, could best be handled here in the club. Dr. Gregg here"—he indicated the famous Alienist—"has some ideas on how we may—"

The Doctor interjected: "You'd better outline the main facts, Rogers. George is impatient—"

"We used that tonic to flavor his drink."

The Banker looked his gratitude.

"I will," agreed the Chemist. "I've sent for the dead woman's immediate family—three of them. And there has been an arrest—the maid, one Ellen Ebert. Sergeant Grantley, of Cliffside, is due here now with her. The facts, gentlemen, are these:

"Anna Crane was an old maid of nearly seventy. An unusual character. As a young woman she went alone to the Yukon. Ran a restaurant or something of the kind, during the gold rush period. Made a small fortune in a few years, selling sandwiches at a dollar each—coffee at fifty cents a cup. You've heard of such things? Well, this woman did it. And took her money and grub-staked two or three down-and-out prospectors. Got control of several rich placer propositions—came out of it all with a fortune of over half a million.

"I knew the woman. Small and frail, with a seamed, rugged face—really rather a genius, a stern but lovable character. She never quite became used to civilization— and of later years was in delicate health. She lived in an unpretentious house, set on the brink of a cliff at Cliffside. Lived down there winter and summer, with one loyal old maidservant—this Ellen Ebert—herself a spinster of fifty odd.

"The death occurred late last month—the evening of September 5. Miss Crane's only close relatives—her dead sister's husband and two grown children—lived with her during the summer. They were in Jamaica this evening. Miss Crane and her maid were alone in the cottage.

"The family returned about eleven thirty. They found the house undisturbed. The servant was asleep in her own room. A light was burning in Miss Crane's bedroom. This was unusual. Miss Crane was a methodical woman—her unchangeable daily routine was almost an obsession. And the maid was equally methodical.

"Each of them did exactly the same things at the same time each day. Miss Crane's bedtime was nine o'clock. The family, seeing the unusual light, went to her bedroom. They found her lying on the floor in her nightdress. Dead!"

2

"**THE MAID WAS** awakened. By the family's testimony of what occurred during the hour before Sergeant Grantley arrived, Ellen Ebert appeared wholly innocent. Horrified—grief-stricken at the loss of her beloved mistress. She said she and Miss Crane had retired to their separate rooms at nine o'clock. Miss Crane was in her usual health seemingly; and was acting in no way peculiar. The maid is very slightly deaf. She says she fell asleep at once—knew nothing until the family awakened her with news of the tragedy."

"You said she died of prussic acid poisoning," the Bacteriologist suggested.

"Yes. A glance at the body—its contorted face—was enough to indicate a violent death. The family left everything untouched and sent for the police. They all thought it was an accident; they maintain she was not the type who would commit suicide.

"To be brief, gentlemen, Grantley found a glass of water on the small table which stood by the side of the bed. A glass half filled with a sheet of paper over it and a teaspoon lying on top. The way medicine sometimes stands in a sick room. Ellen Ebert says it was not there, to her memory, earlier that evening. Nor had the family ever seen it before. Miss Crane was taking no doctor's prescription.

"She was not ill—was not under a doctor's care. She was, however, in the habit of constantly talking mild remedies—tonics, ordinary drug store medicines, harmless and not particularly powerful.

"This glass of water at the bedside, with its teaspoon suggesting that it was a medicine, was something new to the family and the maid. It looked ominous and they did not touch it. It was indeed ominous! It was found to contain hydrocyanic acid—a solution sufficiently strong so that a tea-spoonful of it would cause death inevitably in a very few minutes."

"But," demanded the Banker, "does that mean she took it accidentally? Or did one of them give it to her in the guise of medicine? If somebody did that—why leave the glass right there as evidence?"

The Chemist shrugged. "Left it there possibly to indicate accidental death, or suicide. At all events, it was there. And the autopsy showed death by that poison. Ellen Ebert was arrested. She was alone in the house with Miss Crane. She had every opportunity to administer the poison. And she—in common with the three members of the family—was an heir. If it were murder—well, it's fairly obvious that money furnished the motive.

"I'll pass that aspect of it for a moment. Mr. Blaine questioned the servant after her arrest. She broke down utterly, but, nevertheless, protested complete innocence. Blaine later discussed the poison with me. Hydrocyanic acid—known popularly as prussic acid—is one of the most energetic of poisons. In fluid form it is limpid and volatile, with an odor of bitter almonds. It is very soluble in water and alcohol. Easily administered, either for murder, suicide, or taken by mistake. Death results, I should say, in from two to forty minutes, depending upon the quantity taken. That's so, isn't it, Dr. Adams?"

"Yes," agreed the Doctor.

"You gentlemen can apply these facts to the case in hand," the Chemist went on, "and theorize quite as we have. Further: Mr. Blaine, in questioning the maid, could only determine that she acted wholly innocent. Also, there was one other thing peculiar at the scene of the crime. Miss Crane's bedroom had a private bath adjoining. In the bathroom was her medicine cabinet. Sergeant Grantley found this cabinet partially emptied of its accustomed bottles.

"The maid and the family testified to what bottles had been there. The usual household remedies—the antiseptic for cuts, the tonic, the bromide—which I've already mentioned. And bicarbonate of soda, aromatic spirits of ammonia—that sort of thing. Well, most of them were gone from the cabinet.

"The bathroom window was closed. This window faces the cliff—is right over the brink of it, in fact. Not the ocean here. An inlet, with a narrow, muddy beach. It suggested that the missing articles of the cabinet could easily have been thrown through this window down into the water. A search later that night which Sergeant Grantley conducted in secret, resulted in the establishment of this theory as a fact.

"He found a sodden box of bicarbonate of soda—a broken bottle of aromatic spirits of ammonia. Quite evidently the missing articles from the cabinet were thrown through the bathroom window. The tide was going out that evening. Most of the bottles which remained intact and which chanced to have in them a small enough quantity of liquid, would float and be carried out to sea—and thus be lost to us.

"This discovery brought a new aspect to the affair. It seemed to eliminate accidental death and suicide as probabilities. Because a woman taking poison by mistake, or committing suicide, isn't apt to throw bottles from a window. Thus we turned to murder as most likely. And, in the case of murder, we were led to rather curious deductions, which—"

"Mr. Rogers, Sergeant Grantley is here." A club attendant stood in the doorway. "And those other people arrived ten minutes ago—I've been holding them outside as you ordered."

"Oh—yes. Sergeant Grantley—and someone with him?"

"Yes, sir. A woman."

"And three other visitors ten minutes ago?"

"Yes, sir. A Mr. Rollins, and his son and daughter. I told them to wait—"

"Good. Well, bring them all in at once. Now."

The door closed. The Chemist said hastily: "With Dr. Gregg's experiment—we're going to try it on them at once—we feel sure—"

"Wait," exclaimed the Banker. "One question, Rogers. Those bottles thrown from the window—you found one or two of them? One of them contained poison? Is that it?"

The Chemist shook his head. "No. Not one of them had any trace of poison. The only poison we found was in that glass of water at the bedside."

"Then why in Heaven's name would anyone throw bottles from—"

The door opened again. The visitors entered—Detective Sergeant Grantley, with his prisoner, Ellen Ebert, the maid; and the three relatives of the dead woman.

Ellen Ebert, as the Chemist had said, was a woman something over fifty. Plain of feature and of dress. A frail, shriveled figure—a typical old maid housekeeper and "companion." She sat near Sergeant Grantley, after gazing silently at the group of scientists. Her demeanor was downcast; slightly sullen, yet rather more with the outward aspect of being overwhelmed at this plight into which she had fallen.

The three members of the family entered amid a confusion of introductions and greetings. George Rollins was the dead woman's brother-in-law—a widower who had married Miss Crane's younger sister. He was a big, florid man of extreme geniality; the hail-fellow-well-met type, who obviously prided himself on being a good mixer.

His two children—Miss Crane's niece and nephew— were twins, now twenty-two years old. A pretty girl, this Violet Rollins. Blue eyed, and with fluffy bobbed hair. Yet a girl of intellect, suggesting a mother of good birth and breeding. Her mother had been dead for some eight years; the girl was a curious mixture of her mother's refinement and her father's flashy loudness.

Michael Rollins, her brother, was slim and blond, with a very small light blond mustache. A dapper youth, reserved and dignified as though with a consciousness of his own superiority. Carefully dressed; straight hair slicked back as though with grease. Both he and Violet were college graduates; and the knowledge of the superiority it gave them showed plainly in their manners.

3

WHEN THE VISITORS were seated, the Chemist addressed them. "We won't detain you long. We are, as you know, seeking to reach some conclusion in the death of Miss Crane. This woman here—" He indicated Ellen Ebert.

"She isn't guilty of any murder," boomed George Rollins. He sat at his ease in a leather chair, and flung back the lapels of his coat, a pudgy hand toying with the watch chain which crossed his expansive vest. "Never would have murdered that fine little woman, my sister-in-law. Why, Mr. Rogers, we all loved Anna Crane. Ellen loved her. You're making a mistake—"

The Chemist's gesture checked him. "Possibly so, Mr. Rollins. We know you can't believe murder was done—"

"Not by Ellen. I don't know anything about whether it was murder or not, but—"

Violet said caustically: "You talk too much, father! Why don't you let *him* say something? He didn't send for us to hear your theories."

Rollins grinned at her good-naturedly, and said to the Chemist: "My weakness, Mr. Rogers. You see my children are on to me." He sighed heavily. "These precocious children—"

The son said quietly: "Father merely means, Mr. Rogers, that we, none of us, believe Ellen would be guilty of murder.

We all loved Aunt Anna—and Ellen was like one of the family." The young man spoke with quiet conscious dignity. "In other words, if you've sent for us to help Ellen get off—"

The Chemist nodded emphatically. "That's it, exactly." He smiled at the maid as though to convince her of his friendliness and the sincerity of his words. "We of the Scientific Club, as you perhaps know, very often join with the authorities in the solution of problems which cannot be solved by routine methods. This is such a case. I may as well tell you at once, the police are really undecided. This is confidential, you understand. They may perhaps be able to convict Miss Ebert—"

The maid had been listening closely. She shrank in her chair at this statement from the Chemist and said vehemently: "I'm not guilty, I tell you! I don't know anything about—"

"One moment, please. I'm talking now absolutely frank. Whether we believe Miss Ebert guilty or not, our *belief* has nothing to do with it. Justice requires that she be convicted if it is possible with the evidence we have against her. You understand that, don't you? Personally, I am of the opinion that Miss Crane took the poison by accident. I don't know how it happened, but that's what I believe."

Rollins settled himself as though for genial argument. "Well now, assume—"

"If you please!" The Chemist was smiling. "No doubt I'm as verbose as your children claim you are. But I'll be through in a moment.

"We feel—we of the club here—that very possibly we can prove Miss Crane died an accidental death. A rather unusual mode of procedure—this we propose to use. Occultism—supernatural—"

His words surprised them, and fairly terrified the maid. The Chemist laughed. "Wait a moment! You won't find it very awe-inspiring, or frightening in the slightest. Ordinarily no such evidence would be acceptable in court. Yet from the Scientific Club—properly attested by these gentlemen as witnesses—it might carry considerable weight."

Rollins said: "Well now, that's interesting, Mr. Rogers. Of course you know, I don't take any stock in spirits—except in liquid form." He laughed heartily at the time-worn pun.

Violet murmured to her brother: "That's a lotta apple sauce—spiritualism!"

Michael whispered: "Yeh. Bunk. Shut up now. Let's hear him."

The Chemist was continuing: "You have perhaps heard of our Professor Gregg—" He indicated the Alienist. "Professor Gregg has devoted most of his life to the study of spiritualism—I might say his fame is worldwide."

Several of the club members smiled involuntarily at this misstatement concerning the Alienist, but the smiles and surprised murmurs passed unnoticed. George Rollins gazed at the Alienist with interest, seemingly mixed with awe. The two young people regarded him with faint, somewhat supercilious smiles.

The Chemist went on: "Professor Gregg is about to try an experiment upon one of you three—which one it will be for him to determine. He will leave Miss Ebert out of this. You can understand—assuming we might get some testimony from 'over the border'—if it came through Miss Ebert, testimony in her favor, the authorities would doubtless consider it somewhat prejudiced. But any one of you three will be conceded as a perfectly unbiased outsider. You understand?"

They nodded. George Rollins said pleasantly: "We'll help all we can, of course. Although I'm free to confess this supernatural stuff isn't—I say, this isn't going to be *too* spooky, is it? I never did like—"

"Not at all," smiled the Chemist. "Professor Gregg will explain. Professor, will you continue this?"

"Yes, Mr. Rogers." The Alienist stood up, and for a moment gazed quietly about the room. He was a tall, spare man in his sixties—gray-haired, with a lean long face, smooth-shaven, and a deep, pleasant voice. He stood regarding the visitors, eying them fixedly as though trying to gauge them. Rollins smiled a little nervously. Violet giggled, and her brother murmured a vehement "Shut up!"

"A quite unusual experiment," the Alienist began. "It may or may not result in anything." He advanced to the center table, drawing a chair up after him, and seating himself under the electrolier. A pad of paper and pencil lay on the table, also four or five large, heavy books.

In the silence of the room he resumed: "It is futile for me to try and explain the exact nature of this experiment. The theories of spiritualism are not readily explainable. I take it all three of you loved Miss Crane very much?"

They gazed at each other; then murmured assent.

"And she loved all of you?"

Again they nodded, and he went on: "I want to use one of you three as a medium—the one whom Miss Crane in life loved the most. Through that one now she would be most likely to communicate. I need also a person with a certain type of mentality—a certain powerful intellectual force is necessary."

He stopped and again seemed measuring them. "I believe I will have to experiment first to judge which of you is best qualified intellectually." He appeared thinking deeply. "You have no objection, I suppose, to having your intellect measured?"

Rollins laughed. "Heavens no! But you'll find me awful dumb."

To the young people this was more interesting. Fresh from college this sort of thing was more understandable. They smiled at the Alienist as though keenly confident of their intellect.

"What's the idea?" Michael demanded. "Some kind of a questionnaire?"

The Alienist shook his head. "No. A simple parlor game. And it's a good index to keenness of intellect, deductive powers and general ability to reason. We'll try it. It goes like this."

He selected one of the bulky books and opened it on his knee. "I select from the encyclopedia an article describing something with which I'm sure you are all familiar. I read aloud to you, and you are to guess what I'm reading about. I skip around in the article. At first I disguise the thing. Then I describe it more plainly, until you cannot help getting it. In reading, when I come to the exact word which you are to guess I say blank. And if I come to words too closely allied to it so that by mentioning them I'd give it away I say dash. Like this—it's really quite easy to do."

4

HE SELECTED THE article *coal,* and read, " *'Blank is one of the most important of minerals.'* The *blank* stands for *coal,* you see? *'It consists chiefly of dash and is universally regarded as of vegetable origin.'* The *dash* is the word *carbon*—I left it out for fear of making it too plain at the start. I go on reading like that. If no one guesses correctly I might jump back to the start and read: *'Blank in the sense of a piece of glowing fuel.'* By that time one of you would certainly have it."

"Not me," declared Rollins lugubriously. "These young people. I've forgotten all my book learning."

"It isn't book learning," the Alienist declared. "If fairly simple, commonplace things are chosen it's a question of the reasoning powers of the mind. You get several disjointed facts—you piece them together, deducting what the answer *must* be. And the speed of the mental processes is a factor—or else someone will get ahead of you and guess it first—especially when the reader suddenly makes it very plain and you only have a second or two to shout out the answer."

He rehearsed the rules of the game—the score, minus one for a wrong guess, plus five for a right guess, and the game plus twenty-five—until the three contestants signified that they understood thoroughly. Rollins maintained laughingly that he was beaten before he started. Violet and

Michael seemed interested and still confident of their ability. They all three took it lightly enough. But the scientists, understanding more clearly the Alienist's purpose, were watching and listening keenly.

"Are you ready?" The Alienist selected a volume, thumbed the pages, and began to read:

" *'Thus does the blank, to say nothing of its maritime relations.'* You see, I'm starting in the middle—*'maritime relations bring its inland navigation—'* "

"Ship!" called Violet impulsively.

"Minus one," declared the Alienist. He jotted down the number against her name. "You're too hasty." He read on:

" *'A tremendous developing influence on every country, Chili alone excepted—'* "

"South America!" Rollins blurted out. He looked sheepish as the Alienist scored him minus one. The Alienist commented: "You didn't reason on that at all. This *blank*, I said, was a *developing influence*. Keep that fact in mind until you get some further knowledge to add to it—*'Steamboat navigation began on the blank in 1853.'* Now then! Look out—it's coming! *'Blank, a river which, after traversing nearly the entire breadth of South America—'* "

"Amazon!" Rollins shouted. And, to the chagrin of the young people, the Alienist scored him plus five. The next word was *ice*. Michael guessed wrongly twice and then hit it just ahead of Violet, who had also guessed wrongly twice.

"All right," said the father. "I'm still ahead. I'm going to play conservative. Let's have another. I say, Dr. Gregg—this is interesting—but are we getting anywhere? Has this got anything to do with helping to get Ellen off this murder charge? I suppose you scientists know what you're about—it sounds sort of foolish to—"

"We're not wasting time," the Alienist said smilingly. "Now then, here's a short, quick one! *'Blank has very powerful sedative qualities—'* "

"Tobacco!"—from Michael.

"Not bad, but wrong. *'As a sedative in sleeplessness its use produces beneficial results—'* "

There was a long pause. Then Violet guessed: "Bromide!"

"Good enough! That's correct.

Rollins said: "I had a hunch it was bromide—I was waiting for more facts to be sure."

The game went on. They had *music, soda, United States, Lloyd George, aromatic spirits of ammonia, tonic*—widely diverse words intermingled. The contestants seemed enthusiastic and alert. Yet to the silent observers it seemed as though gradually a sense of danger were awakening in the players.

If it were, they were intelligent enough to realize it must be disguised. Intelligent enough, doubtless, so that from the first a realization might have been with them that this was some trap. Yet, if so, the guilty one obviously knew that an outward show of perturbation or reluctance would be most dangerous of all.

5

MORE THAN HALF an hour was consumed. The game ended with Rollins winning at twenty-seven; Violet and Michael tied at twenty-three. One or two of the words the Alienist had used twice—disguising them by reading completely different facts concerning them. And in each case Rollins guessed them both times.

The Surgeon whispered to the Doctor beside him: "He's got it, Adams—whatever it is!"

"Yes—I think so. Sh!"

The Alienist was saying: "Unfortunately a close game like that—not a bit conclusive of which of you I need for my psychic experiment." He glanced at his watch. "I think we would not have time for another game."

"Why not use all three of them," the Chemist suggested. "If a message from the dead woman can be received it will come through one of them—or even two, possibly."

"Yes," agreed the Alienist. "Dual mediums, simultaneously. I'll start with all three of you. Jack, are you ready?"

The Very Young Man nodded. "Yes, sir. Shall I bring it in now?"

"Yes."

The Very Young Man rose and left the room. His obvious excitement communicated itself to the three subjects of the forthcoming experiment. They exchanged glances, and taking the cue one from the other, were all dubious of their willingness to proceed.

But the Alienist insisted. Told them it was nothing to be afraid of. Nothing spooky. No stage trickery, as with the professional spiritualists, many of whose séances were faked.

And there was a hint of menace in his voice as he told them that all three of them were regarded by the police and the Scientific Club as mere outsiders in the death of Anna Crane. But a refusal to participate in this harmless experiment might appear very queer to the police. Their position as suspects was but thinly veiled now. All were alarmed. Yet the feeling that spiritualism was nonsense must have made the guilty one smile at such fears. This Professor Gregg—merely a deluded fanatic.

"I'm game," Rollins declared finally. The Very Young Man had a moment before entered with a cut glass bowl half filled with a clear liquid like water, though slightly tinged with color. Rollins eyed the bowl. "I can't say I'm very keen. What's that?" He made a weak attempt at jocularity. "Isn't booze, is it?"

"Shut up, father!" adjured Michael. The young man was smiling, but it was a weak, nervous smile. And Violet was staring at the bowl as though fascinated.

The Alienist said: "No, it isn't booze unfortunately. It's a harmless medicine—a little bromide, quinine its main ingredient—diluted with water. In ordinary séances, as you know, the medium and the spectators are put in what they call a quiescent, receptive mood by dim lights, solemn whisperings—all that sort of thing.

"That is largely stage atmosphere—merely to be impressive. But not altogether so. A relaxed, receptive mood is absolutely necessary. This can be obtained, not so dramatically, but far more effectively, by the use of certain harmless medicines. It is this method which we scientific men—caring nothing for dramatics—prefer to use. This liquid—a glass of it—"

"I won't take it," Violet exclaimed. "The idea—"

The Chemist, who had been sitting quietly listening to what the Alienist had been saying, jumped to his feet. "What nonsense! Professor Gregg assures you it's harmless. So do I. Why a quart of it wouldn't hurt you! All in that bowl—"

The Doctor interjected: "All in the bowl would give a person a few hours of restful sleep. Perhaps make the head ring a little from the quinine. But a single glass—"

The Chemist had left his chair and gone to the bowl. Smilingly he dipped up a glassful of the liquid and drank it. "You see? Perfectly harmless—and the taste is quite pleasant."

"I don't," Rollins began.

"Absolutely harmless," the Alienist reiterated. "You Jack—drink a glassful."

The Very Young Man did so unhesitatingly. And so did the Alienist. And the Alienist reiterated once more: "Harmless—and the medicinal effect is hardly noticeable. Yet, though you cannot realize they are doing so, these mild medicines relax your nerves. Isn't that so, Dr. Adams?"

They were persuaded finally. Rollins dipped up his glassful, hesitated, and with a look of grim, desperate determination, gulped it down. The Very Young Man passed glasses to Michael and Violet. The girl drank hers, partially, and then finished it. And Michael, after a preliminary taste, drank his.

"Well," said Rollins, "that wasn't so—"

"Pleasant enough, wasn't it?" the Alienist smiled. "Now just sit quiet—let yourselves relax." He added casually: "For technical reasons we wanted this potion to contain a flavoring well liked by Miss Crane. She often took various harmless remedies. Queerly enough, as you know, her medicine cabinet had been rifled. We wanted the actual bottles—and we found some of them."

He was speaking very rapidly now, but quietly as though his words were of no great importance. "You didn't know that, did you? The bottles were thrown through the bathroom window. We found one of them fortunately intact—and we used its contents to flavor this drink—Miss Crane's beef, iron and wine tonic. That accounts for the slightly bitter but certainly pleasant enough taste."

"You fool! My God—"

"That tonic! In *this?* Why he—he's killed us—and himself—killed us all!" Violet's hysterical scream. She was on her feet, her brother Michael with her, his face chalk-white.

"You fool!" He shouted it at the Alienist, and then stood stupidly horrified, clinging to his sister, gulping, and with beads of sweat coming to his forehead.

"Hey, for Heaven's sake, what's the idea?" Rollins was up with them, his face puzzled and alarmed. "What's the matter with you two?"

"A doctor!" gasped Violet. "That fool—killed us all—in a minute we'll all be—"

The detective leaped at them. "What is it? Michael, what is it?"

"Poison! That—that tonic of hers—don't you realize it—that's what killed her—and now we've—"

And Violet crying incoherently: "That tonic—we've all taken it—it had prussic acid in it! That was what killed her! And now we—*don't* stand there like that! Get us something! Do something! In a minute or two—God, it's too late now—"

Hysterical, both of them; wildly calling for medical aid; and both of them confessing fully. And it was not until they were convinced that Miss Crane's tonic was *not* in the drink they had taken that they realized they had been trapped.

When, later, the room had quieted, the Chemist said: "A trap of this kind, gentlemen, when the conditions are right, seldom fails of its purpose. Dr. Gregg wished to use it in this case—it comes so suddenly—it threatens so much, that its victim never has time to reason, or to guard against it. Dr. Gregg felt sure that if he could use it we would be successful. Its merit also lies in the fact that two or more criminals may be caught with it at once. It separates the innocent from the guilty with surprising swiftness and clarity.

"We had, however, an obstacle to using it—in this case—an obstacle which Dr. Gregg had to overcome first. From the beginning we felt that that glass of water with its prussic acid was a blind. Principally because the spoon on top of the glass had no poison on it. And the poison in the glass had not reached above the line of the surface of the liquid as it would have were the elderly Miss Crane to have sipped any of it.

"We assumed then that the glass of poison was put there to incriminate Miss Ebert—and the criminal added the spoon as a lifelike touch, but forgot to dip the spoon in the glass. If, then, Miss Ebert were innocent, the poison must have been placed in some medicine which Miss Crane habitually took. And thus she would administer it to herself on this evening when the criminal was absent.

"This theory was helped by the fact that the medicine cabinet was emptied. What actually happened, we find now, is this: These two young college graduates—'young intellectuals' their prototypes were notoriously termed recently—planned to murder their aunt. Both were of age—both would come immediately into their very large inheritance.

"They knew that prussic acid was highly soluble in the liquid tonic, and that the taste would not be noticed. They knew that Miss Ebert would be in her own room, and that she is somewhat deaf. And that their aunt would die in a few moments after taking her accustomed tablespoon of the tonic.

"They came home with their father. In the haste and confusion following the discovery of the body it was not difficult for one of them to plant the glass of poison—and for the other hastily to throw the bottles out of the bathroom window. It was necessary to get rid of that poisonous tonic. They knew if only the tonic were missing it would be suspected as possibly being poisoned. So they threw out most of the bottles to confuse the issue.

"And since then they have been acting what they considered normally innocent. Their father refused to believe Miss Ebert guilty—wanted to help her get off. And they were clever enough to see that it would be safest for them to appear anxious for the same outcome.

"Our own problem was to lay this trap. But we could not do it without knowing which of Miss Crane's remedies had carried the poison. The bottles which we found did not have any trace of poison. The tonic and some of the others we did not find.

"Dr. Gregg's game is really a very fascinating parlor diversion, as he said. It is also a very good and quite simple psychological test. He used many innocent words. But he also used each of the missing medicines. After a word or two Dr. Gregg was able to classify the deductive powers of each of the three mentalities. Rollins guessed at every word with what was for him perfectly normal deductions.

"Michael and Violet did not. They very soon scented danger. They became inwardly confused—frightened—not knowing what the thing meant at all—fearful that they would give some of their guilty knowledge away. Even a person less trained in psychology than Dr. Gregg could observe the abnormality of their answers. Both Violet and Michael are more nimble-minded, more logical-minded, more learned than their father.

"Playing the game ordinarily, he would not have a chance with them. But the reading about those medicines disturbed Michael and Violet, and their answers during the reading of the word tonic, most conspicuously of all, failed to show the normal deductions of which—as proven by their reactions to the innocuous words—their minds were capable.

"And so Dr. Gregg determined that the poison had been the tonic. He named the tonic then as the flavoring ingredient of our drink, and—well, gentlemen, had any of us been in their place I believe we would have acted about as they did."

THE CURIOUS CASE
OF ADRIAN LLOYD

"IT IS A clear case of abnormal memory," said the Doctor. "Mr. Lloyd is, in that sense, *living backward.*"

The Doctor gazed at the intent group of men around him. "Understand me, gentlemen, Mr. Lloyd has been greatly harassed by his mental condition. It is a terrible thing for a strong, normally balanced man to become convinced that his reason is shaken."

The Doctor turned slightly. Beside him sat a stranger to the club—a slim but muscular-looking man of about thirty-five. His English birth and breeding were apparent in his clothes and demeanor, as well as in his intonation when presently he spoke. His hair was blond, his eyes a mild blue. They were worried eyes; and over the normally ruddy tinge of his complexion a pallor had settled. The Doctor met his gaze, and the man smiled. But it was a harassed, almost a frightened, smile.

"A disturbing—a terrible thing," the Doctor repeated. "He came to me, and together we consulted Eastland."

At this mention of his name, the noted Alienist across the room nodded. "Queer case," he murmured to the man beside him. "Damned queer; and yet—"

"Is he going to tell us about it?" demanded the Very Young Man, in an excited whisper. "I mean, this Lloyd himself. I want to hear him tell it."

"Hush, boy!" growled the Banker.

The Doctor caught the Very Young Man's words. "I have asked Mr. Lloyd to tell you gentlemen just what he has told me. I have no selfish purpose in putting him through such an ordeal merely for the enlightenment of us here at the club. I believe—and so does Eastland—that the actual telling will do him good—will help straighten him out."

Again the Doctor met their visitor's eyes. He added gently: "You have kept this to yourself too closely, Mr. Lloyd. Turning it over in your own head—dwelling on it alone—the thing has become an obsession. You are perfectly sane"—he smiled slightly; "that is to say, as near to perfect sanity as anyone of us ever is. Believe that, Mr. Lloyd, for if you don't—well, you will head yourself for the very thing you fear most. There is no mentality strong enough to stand up against a genuine belief that it is tottering."

"Easy enough to give advice like that," murmured the Astronomer to his neighbor. "But, God, man—that chap's frightened! Frightened right down to the core of him! Watch his fingers—he can't keep them still."

The Doctor was continuing. "No one could have a more sympathetic audience than you gentlemen. Mr. Lloyd has to tell you of a woman he loved very deeply—his wife—"

"A girl!" the Very Young Man whispered. He was thrilled.

"—his wife, now dead—and you gentlemen will understand, and sympathize in a way that leaves him free to tell you his closest feelings." The Doctor was addressing Lloyd directly. "I want you to do that, Mr. Lloyd. Get it all out of your mind now. Everything. It will help you. It may even dispel this illusion entirely."

There was a brief pause, but Lloyd did not speak.

"You said he was living backward," the Banker suggested out of a silence. "What do you mean by that? You mean his memory is—"

The Doctor raised his hand. "Just a minute, George." He turned to Lloyd again. "You will tell them—what you told Eastland and me?"

"Yes." The man's twitching hands came up to his knees, then went to the arms of his big leather chair, which he hitched forward nervously. "Yes—I'll try.... Turn that light away, please. It—it bothers me."

The Doctor tipped the brown parchment shade of the table electrolier down on one side. The room, with wall lights out, was largely in shadow. The table light threw an oval of illumination on the men nearest it. The edge of it crossed Lloyd's chest; his lean hands, with fingers that strove to keep from twisting, were in the light; his face was in the shadow. There was a brown-paper parcel in the chair with him; one of his hands went down to it, fumbled aimlessly with the string.

"It started almost a year ago," Lloyd began softly. "Almost a year ago—within a month or two after my wife's—my wife's death." He spoke in a halting monotone, but presently he seemed to force himself to more composure.

"I married an American girl. Her name was Ellen Rance—we were married here in New York. She had no relatives—I mean to say, none around here, except an aunt who died soon after we were married. We went to the Orient for our honeymoon."

His hand beside him came up to his lap, bringing the paper parcel. Evidently it contained some heavy object;

he rested it on his knees; his fingers twitched at its string, but did not undo it. And there was stamped plainly in his manner and on his face an aversion from, a repugnance to this thing on his lap.

The Very Young Man leaned forward. "What's he got there? What is it?" But the Banker silenced him with a gruff whisper.

"Ellen was happy—I thought very happy. One day—we were stopping in Benares—she came back to our hotel with something she had purchased. She was acting queerly. I remember I thought so at the time. Nervous—but, gentlemen, she was always very nervous. High-strung, I always called it—for she was a thoroughbred, a real thoroughbred. You could tell that by the slimness of her—those delicate features. She was brown-haired and blue-eyed—very beautiful, I thought; and so did everyone else."

"She had purchased something," the Doctor prompted.

"Yes. And when she came in with it, I was struck with her heightened color." Lloyd's voice rose suddenly. "More than that, gentlemen, there was something in her eyes—some queer look, I mean to say—that frightened me. Let it pass. You will think it is only my imagination now, because of what happened afterward. She had purchased, in Benares that afternoon—this."

His fingers jerked, opened the package. The paper wrappings dropped to the floor, and, hurriedly, as though to avoid a repulsive physical contact, he placed a heavy green object on the table. The light from the electrolier shone down full upon it. The men leaned forward expectantly.

The thing seemed a table or a mantel ornament. It was of polished green jade—a jagged rock in the hollow of which a snake was coiled. The snake's head was upraised to strike; its jeweled eyes caught the light and seemed to gleam balefully. Behind the snake, a little fat-bellied figure in human form squatted on the rock and smiled down on the reptile approvingly. The whole was a conventional bit of carving, yet there was about it an intangible look of power, of mystery. It may have been the solid green of the jade; to a first glance, as though by protective coloring, the green snake and green figure on that green rock were hardly visible. Or there may have been inherent in the moulded lines that queer inscrutability of the Orient, which to Occidental minds seems sinister. Whatever it was, it was there—that sense of mystery and power—and every man in the room felt it within a moment.

"She purchased—that," Lloyd repeated. His voice held both fear and abhorrence. "She told me it possessed an Oriental charm for beneficence. That grinning figure there on the rock—it's supposed to be watching the snake strike at Evil, or some such rot. Beneficence! It—it's cursed, gentlemen. I'd have destroyed it long ago, only I—well, I can't seem to bring myself to do it."

He laughed a little wildly, in spite of an effort to steady himself. "Those emerald snake eyes fascinate me, if you want to call it that. I told Dr. Adams it's because I'm—I'm irrational now. I confessed it to him—I'll confess it to all of you. Since that—that thing killed Ellen, I sit staring at it sometimes for hours at a time. I mean to say, I know it will finish me up, too, someday. That's its beneficence! To get me out of this—and a good, kindly job, too!"

"Unbalanced," the Astronomer murmured. "He knows he is, and fears it. That's what he's afraid of."

"No," contradicted the Alienist softly. "Not unbalanced as you mean it. Not insanity. Obsessed by grief—the tragedy of his wife's death—you'll hear in a moment. And something else. *I* don't understand it, if you come to that. I'm damned if I do."

The Doctor was endeavoring to quiet Lloyd. The man obviously was under tremendous tension—an hysteria which threatened every moment to break through his efforts to control it.

"I'll go on," Lloyd resumed presently. "I can—tell you everything perfectly calmly if I once make up my mind to it. I—I got to hating that damned thing you see there on the table. But Ellen insisted on having it around. The man who sold it to her told her something about it—a legend or something. She let that out once, but she would never tell me *what* it was he said. Some selling talk, I fancy. But, God! How queer she looked when I questioned her about it. Angry. But frightened, too. And a hunted, haunted look in her eyes.

"We came back to New York—took an apartment here. She kept that damned idol on the mantel. It could easily have fallen off—cracked someone on the head. Several times I put it on the table. It was in our bedroom—she *would* have it there where that cursed snake would wake me up with its green eyes staring at me in the light of dawn…. But she never failed to replace it on the mantel when I moved it."

Lloyd's gaze was on the green snake as he spoke. It seemed to cling there against his will. Occasionally he would shift it to the faces of his silent little audience, but always it drifted back.

"One night I came home fagged out from working late. It was just after we had found Ellen was—was to be a mother. I came upon her in our bedroom. She was kneeling before this thing as though it were an idol. She sprang up when I spoke to her and faced me. And again—and this time, gentlemen, it was absolutely unmistakable—I saw in her eyes that haunted look of terror. She looked as though she were afraid of something—trying to escape from something. I don't know what. I never found out. I fancy now I never shall; but I wish—I wish to God I could know what haunted her all those happy months of her marriage."

Lloyd's voice trailed away. The men sat silent, most of them staring at the gleaming green jeweled eyes of the jade snake. The room was hushed save for the slow ticking of a huge clock in the corner.

"Yes?" prompted the Doctor at last.

Lloyd started. "Oh, yes; what was I saying?" He smiled wanly and locked his fingers together in his lap to hold them quiet. "I was drifting, Dr. Adams. *You* know. It's hard, even here with all these people, to keep myself straight."

"You were telling us of the night you quarreled," the Doctor said gently.

"Quarreled? Yes—that was when we quarreled. She had been kneeling to this damned idol. I was fagged out, I tell you. I fancy my nerves were on edge, too. She had this jade thing on the very brink of the bedroom mantel, and she was kneeling under it—praying to it, I think.

"It made me shudder. And I was angry; and when she met my remonstrances with anger as hot as my own, we— we quarreled. I won't give you details. I said things for which I shall never forgive myself. Only one thing I must repeat. I told her she was acting and talking like a crazy woman—unbalanced—and I think I added that evidently all women were unbalanced more or less.

"It silenced her when I said that. She stood looking at me dumbly. I don't want to excuse myself to you gentlemen. I acted like a brute. I haven't a rag of excuse, and that— that's the terrible part of it. I had forgotten our baby was coming—forgotten that for a man to lose his temper, speak angrily to his wife at such a time. . . .

"I slammed out of the room. I think it was in my mind I would pass the night in my study. I lay down on my couch—tried to go to sleep. But I couldn't. The maid was asleep—the place was silent. But I could hear Ellen's footsteps as she paced the floor of the bedroom. Once she stopped. The silence terrified me; but in a minute I could hear her again—back and forth.

"I don't know how much time went by; but my anger cooled; I was filled with contrition and remorse. If only Ellen would forgive me—forget my words. I loved her more than anything else in the world.

"I was in the hall, on my way to our bedroom. Ellen was silent in there. Then I heard a moan, and something fell—a thud, limp, muffled by the closed bedroom door.

"I found Ellen lying on the floor in there—dead! That— that damned thing you see there had killed her. But it wasn't accidental. It had not fallen on her, because she was too far from the mantel for that. This—jade thing was in her hand. She had struck her head with it—crashed it down on her head with a blow that killed her!" There followed another heavy silence.

"Suicide," murmured one of the men.

Lloyd raised his white face. "Yes. A suicide. And, gentlemen, I was responsible for that. My angry, hot-tempered words killed her, and—and our child, as surely as though I had struck them down with my own hand. That's what's the matter with me—that's the thing that is driving me mad. I can't stand the thought of it, and I won't—much longer."

"Frank, you *said* he was living backward," the Banker insisted in a whisper. "What did you mean? He hasn't spoken of that."

"Memories," answered the Doctor. "His memories—wait, you'll hear."

Lloyd had fallen again into that apathy with which he seemed always struggling. He roused himself at the words.

"Memories! Yes. That's the crux of it now. After Ellen's death this—this other thing came on me. It came suddenly. I was sitting staring at that idol. I was thinking of all the different events of our honeymoon—how gentle and sweet Ellen always was—and yet how there seemed to be something hanging over her—tearing at her nerves—secretly, so that she would never even admit it to me.

"This particular afternoon, as I sat there lost in reverie, was when I first knew that since Ellen's death something had gone wrong with my head. You all know how, for an hour or two, you can drift along in memories—lose yourself in living them over again, vividly—as vividly almost as the original reality? I was doing that when suddenly I became conscious that it was dinner-time. I was alone in my bedroom at the British-American Club. I live there altogether, now—I've given up the apartment.

"I knew I was hungry and dinner was on downstairs.

But beyond that knowledge I could not arouse myself. It was like a dream in which you know you are dreaming and want to wake up, but cannot.

"They were—they are now—not like regular memories. Normal memories are jumbled—you leap about in them from one event to another. But these are consecutive. That afternoon and evening I was living over again a day with Ellen when we were in New York after our honeymoon—a day just a little while before her death. Every trivial incident of it was coming back to me vividly—so vividly that it seemed the reality; and the fact that I was sitting alone, a widower in my club bedroom neglecting his supper, seemed the dream.

"Do I make myself clear to you, gentlemen? I want to—I really want to make myself clear. I felt myself dining again with Ellen in our New York apartment. The conversation we had held—the little caresses—were all repeated. It was not until we had retired, and in my memory I had fallen asleep with my arms around Ellen, that the spell was broken.

"I was released. I found myself sitting in my bedroom chair there at the club. I was cold and stiff. And confused. It was after midnight. I went to bed and slept dreamlessly."

Lloyd was sitting upright in his chair, staring with unseeing eyes at the green jade carving before him. His voice went on in its drab monotone: "That was the beginning. I soon found myself thrown into a sort of dual existence…. These memories crowd into my every waking hour. I can force them away sometimes—just as I am doing now. But when I relax—even for an instant—they rush back upon me."

"You're not making it entirely clear," the Doctor interrupted gently. "Tell them how really consecutive the memories are—and how they are carrying you backward."

"Oh, yes. Thank you, Doctor. I mean to say, gentlemen, every morning when I awaken, the memory of what I did at a very similar time on some other specific morning during my life with Ellen is flooding my mind. All day it is the same—that other day is passing. Often I—I get into a lethargy or something, and just sit and live over that other day until it is finished. I was always a dreamless sleeper. Thank God for that! I am released when the day of my memory has come to its close—and then I can sleep dreamlessly.

"The other thing that Dr. Adams means is that each day in my life now I am living over a day previous in my life with Ellen. Going backward, do you see, to our marriage. I have passed day by day over our return passage from abroad—our stop in England to see my people before we sailed for home; and, still going backward day by day, the memories have reached our stop in India—that very day in Benares when she—"

He checked himself abruptly. "I mean to say, gentlemen—there must be some purpose in all this. I never could quite understand Ellen—and sometimes as I live over these memories I get the idea that they are coming to me so that I might now understand her better. Often I have a detached feeling that enables me to examine them critically. I listen to the memory of the things she used to say to me; I study my mental picture of her as she used to look during those happy days we had in India. It seems now almost as though I had a new insight into things. There was something vital about Ellen that she always held secret from me. I—I sometimes feel that these memories may give me a clue to it—a clue that I overlooked before."

A hush fell over Lloyd's voice as he slowly added: "I almost think, gentlemen, that they are getting to be more than mere memories. Yesterday, for instance, I seemed to become aware of Ellen's *thoughts,* there in Benares. Thoughts she had kept from me at the time. It was all vague—I couldn't grasp it clearly."

Abruptly Lloyd laughed—an eerie laugh that startled several of the men into shifting their feet uneasily. "That's a crazy idea for me to get, isn't it? Dr. Adams and Dr. Eastland try to tell me I am perfectly sane. That's a jest. They think they can talk me out of this thing. For my own good, of course, and I appreciate their efforts. I'm not ungrateful, even if I am—irrational. There's only one way out for me—and that's as easy for me to take as it was for Ellen."

One of the men placed a hand on the Doctor's arm and whispered to him: "That idol oughtn't to be in his possession."

"No, we're going to keep it here," the Doctor responded equally softly. "But today is critical. I thought perhaps we could solve—"

The Astronomer said aloud: "Mr. Lloyd, you hinted that your memories have gone backward now to a day in Benares—" He waited questioningly.

"Yes. I said—what did I say? I—I guess I've forgotten.

The Doctor prompted him again.

"Oh, yes. Doctor. That was it. Today is the day she bought that idol. I've watched this day coming for so long. Been afraid of it. Gentlemen, that's why Dr. Adams brought me here tonight. And this afternoon—he's been talking to me all afternoon to keep my mind off it. This morning my memories took me back to that other day in Benares. But I've kept them away—so I wouldn't—wouldn't have to see her when she bought the idol."

The Alienist spoke up. "Mr. Lloyd, as I understand it, Dr. Adams did not bring you here to have you avoid that memory.... Wait a moment, Doctor, I think we should speak plainly to him.... On the contrary, Mr. Lloyd, we are going to ask you now to let this particular memory into your mind. I want you to relax—let your thoughts dwell on Benares, that time when your wife left you at the hotel and returned a few hours later with this idol, as you call it."

There was a stir in the room as the Alienist added in his measured, sonorous tone: "Will you do that, Mr. Lloyd? We will keep quite silent. We ask only that you repeat aloud the thoughts that come to you."

There followed a brief aside between Lloyd and the Doctor. But Lloyd's protestations were overridden; and the man at last yielded with a hopeless gesture. As the Doctor sat down, Lloyd said querulously: "Won't you *please* turn those lights away from me. Dr. Adams? They—they bother me, I tell you."

There were four bulbs in the table electrolier. The Doctor extinguished all but one of them; the shadows in the room crept up and enveloped Lloyd and all those about him. But the green jade rock was still brightly illumined. Lloyd did not speak, and whispers among the men broke out.

"Silence, gentlemen." It was the Doctor's voice. "Relax, Mr. Lloyd. Lie back in your chair. She is going to buy that idol in a moment. You were at your hotel and didn't know where she went at the time. But now—*see if you can follow her in your thoughts.*"

"God!" murmured the Astronomer. "It he does that—"

Lloyd was already speaking; his voice was so low, so toneless, that even in the hush of the room it was barely audible.

"She is saying good-bye to me that afternoon at the hotel. I think she is going for a stroll. I'm asking her if she wants some money—to buy something, perhaps.... What a queer look! I didn't notice that before. She might be thinking that she's going to buy the idol. She *is* thinking that! Jove! She *is* thinking that!... Now she has left.... I'm watching her from the bedroom window—that squalid, half-naked Hindu beggar, with shriveled legs like sticks—she stops and tosses him a coin.... I can see her—cool, white in her linen as she passes along the crowded street...."

Lloyd's halting phrases left the room in blank silence with each pause. The Doctor said softly, but very tensely:

"Forget yourself. Keep her in sight. Can you?"

"Wait!... Yes, I am with her now—I mean to say I can see her as though I were beside her in the street. She is out of sight of the hotel—turned a corner just this moment. She walks rapidly—her eyes straight before her."

The Alienist's voice came out of the darkness. "Lloyd, what is she thinking? Can't you tell us what her thoughts are?"

"This is no *memory*," the Astronomer whispered in awe. "It's—" But the Alienist silenced him.

"—thinking of something she has determined to buy," Lloyd's voice was saying. "She saw a green jade carving. They told her something about it. The thought frightens her—she won't let her mind dwell on it. That was a week ago. She has been fighting a desire to buy the jade thing—now she is yielding to it."

In the semi-darkness the dim shape of Lloyd's figure showed as he rose suddenly to his feet.

"What's that over there? Dr. Adams, do you see anything? Ellen! Is that you, Ellen?" His voice was shrill—frightened, and yet appealing.

A ripple of confusion swept over the startled listeners. One or two stood up momentarily and glanced around through the shadows. There was no visible presence in the room—every one of the spectators would have sworn to that.

The Doctor drew Lloyd back to his seat. "Nothing, Lloyd."

"No. You're right, Doctor. I thought there was—over there where the window portières are so black.... For a moment I thought she was here. But she isn't; she's just going into a little shop. Yes, there's the damned idol. It's on a shelf. She's walking toward it. I wish—" There was a long pause.

"You wish—what do you wish, Lloyd?" the Doctor prompted gently.

"I wish—wait Doctor, you're wrong. That shadow over there—no, she's moving behind the shadow—behind the wall."

He was turning in his chair; his gaze seemed following something—something which no one but himself could see. But there was a brief instant when each of the men—perhaps by the promptings of his own over-stimulated imagination—felt the presence of the Unknown. Lloyd's breath exhaled audibly; he relaxed in his chair. His voice, when presently he spoke, carried a note of exultation.

"I understand now, gentlemen. Ellen is here with me now. It is she who gives me these memories. She wants me to know something that I never knew—about her and—why she died. Wait! I'll have it in a moment. This old Hindu merchant told her a week ago that jade thing was magic. It cures sickness. The snake is striking at sickness; that is the little God of Health grinning down from the rock. Ellen tells the shop-keeper that is only salesman's talk. But she asks him if the little god and his snake can cure sickness of the mind....

"Why is her heart beating so fast? She is frightened as she smiles at him.... He tells her yes, of course—that is what it chiefly does.... Now he is telling her the legend of the little god and his snake.... Wait!... I fancy he thinks she is a gullible American tourist and she will believe anything.... He says this jade thing once fell and struck a child on the head. That was years ago. The Yogis told him of it. The child was an imbecile—and the blow from the little god *cured it!*"

Lloyd's voice died away, but when the Doctor again prompted him, he said sharply:

"Wait, Doctor! I'll understand it all in a moment. I'm piecing it together—the little things Ellen used to let slip—things that I overlooked before....Oh, I never knew *that* before!"

His voice raised to a cry of anguish. "Doctor! Doctor Adams, she—she thought she was going insane! Her father died of insanity. She never told me—she was afraid to tell me. *That* was why she didn't want us to have a child....

"Ellen—Ellen dear, you should have told me.... She got the idea that she might go insane. And when she found we were going to have a child—she fought against going insane. God! I can understand now how she must have suffered! She bought this damned idol. *That* was irrational—even to consider such rot was irrational. And she knew it—and that frightened her more.

"She used to pray to it in our bedroom when she was alone. She used to wonder—if it *should* fall off the mantel and strike her head, would that cure her? She knew such thoughts were foolish; but the very fact that she could think them seemed proof to her that she was unbalanced.

"Then—that last evening. She was praying to the idol—praying for sanity for herself and her unborn child. And I—I came in and quarreled with her. I told her she was acting and talking like a crazy woman. *A crazy woman!* I didn't mean a thing. God knows—Ellen, *you* know now I didn't mean a thing!

"And when I left her after saying that, a frenzy swept over her. She paced up and down the bedroom trying to fight it. Then she yielded. She took the idol—took it in her little white hand. Suicide! It wasn't that, Doctor. She died with a prayer on her lips that the blow would make her sane. And the blow didn't make her sane. It killed her and her child; and now she knows that the taint was in her—the taint of insanity that would have gone on to the child!"

Lloyd was on his feet and over to the table so quickly that he eluded the Doctor. His laugh rang out.

"It's funny, isn't it, how clear things are when you get all the pieces fitting together? It's all a jest, anyway—life and love and everything!"

The Alienist's cry of warning came from the darkness. Several of the other men shouted. The Doctor was upon Lloyd. But too late. The man had snatched up the jade rock and crashed it against his white forehead. The rock tumbled back to the table. Lloyd's body crumpled, fell in a heap at the Doctor's feet, and lay still.

HE WAS NOT dead, and within an hour they had brought him back to consciousness. Was it chance that in *his* case the blow did not kill? Was it chance that when he recovered they found him freed of those obsessions which had carried him to the brink—or perhaps over the brink—of insanity? And was Lloyd's story all merely the figment of his disordered, obsessed imagination? There is abundant medical precedent for such a coldly scientific explanation.

Or do you prefer the occult interpretation? The idol had killed Lloyd's insane wife and prevented the birth of an idiot child. But Lloyd himself could become of benefit to the world; and the blow from this grinning little God of Health cured him!

Or, again, if you prefer, not Oriental occultism, but American Spiritualism. Let us say that the green jade carving had no occult power. Was it, then, the spirit of Ellen which returned to that room in the Scientific Club? Her husband's mind was on the verge of collapse from grief. He believed his cruel, thoughtless words had driven her to suicide. Perhaps she returned in spirit to set his mind at rest.

You must decide for yourself. The records of the Scientific Club can give you no more than you have just read.

LIGHT OF BETRAYAL

1

THE DIM STUDIO seemed very silent—so silent that Milkin almost fancied he could hear his pounding heart. Lentz was in the adjoining dark-room. Its door was ajar; Lentz was puttering about, getting his plates ready for developing.

Milkin glanced at his watch. Quarter past seven. The time had come! On the mahogany table beside which he was sitting, amid the litter of mounted photographs lying there as samples, was a heavy paperweight of green jade—an Oriental bauble, a solemn-faced green Buddha carved in the jade block, twice the size of a man's fist.

Milkin rose to his feet; stood for an instant to get a grip on himself. His breath was choking him; his forehead was moist and cold; his knees were shaking. That was natural enough, he supposed.

Lentz's voice from the dark-room came startlingly loud through the silence of the rooms. "Rato, how many plates did we make this afternoon?"

"Eight, I think," Milkin answered. His voice was perfectly natural, casual. It calmed him suddenly.

"Yes—I have them all." He heard Lentz shuffling the plate-holders. A moment now and it would all be over.

Milkin seized the green jade Buddha. With it dangling at his side, partially behind him, he moved quietly forward.

Lentz had switched off the studio light. A large, bare room, with canvas scenery looming in the shadows. Canvas reflectors. The portrait camera standing on its wheeled base—standing in the dimness like a shrouded black ghost. To one side, the north skylight through which the lights of nearby buildings filtered with a yellow glow. Through the half-opened dark-room door Milkin could see the radiance of the ruby light by which Lentz was working.

"How do they look?" Still Milkin's voice sounded quite calm. He was advancing now toward the dark-room, with the heavy jade Buddha dangling in his hand.

"A moment, I will have one of them."

So easy, now that Lentz was preoccupied, to come up behind him! Milkin advanced softly. In a moment he was at the doorway to the dark-room. He pushed it open a trifle further. There was no light in the studio that could bother Lentz, even if the dark-room door had been open wide. In the lurid ruby light he saw Lentz selecting a plate-holder. Lentz had his back to the door. Did he realize Milkin was behind him? What matter? An instant now.

Milkin padded forward. The block of jade swung up over Lentz's bended head; crashed down upon it. Lentz's body crumpled, fell in a heap to the floor at the foot of the tank. The plate-holder he had been grasping fell with him. Milkin reeled against the wall, still clinging to the block of jade. He felt sick and trembling; but triumph and relief surged within him. It was over!

In a moment he had again controlled himself. He bent down. Lentz was dead. Crumpled in a heap at the foot of the tank. From a jagged wound in his head blood was welling. Blood that looked almost colorless in this ruby light.

He placed the twelfth stick in the vase and lighted it.

Milkin gathered his scattered wits. No errors now. He must do everything just right. And quickly. Then get out of here. A tumultuous wave of desire possessed him, desire to escape this tiny room—this horrible red glow—that gruesome, crumpled thing on the floor. But he must do everything just right first; and then he could go.

The jade block in his hand might have his fingerprints on it. He washed it in the tank of running water, lifted it gingerly, and placed it in the pool of blood which now was gathered on the floor.

Out in the studio he swiftly unearthed a package he had purchased and hidden there—a package of Chinese incense. They were long sticks of an unfamiliar type—most of them ten inches long and as thick as a man's little finger. There were an even dozen of the sticks. He placed eleven of them in a careless heap on a taboret in the center of the studio. Beside them he stood a small vase; and in the vase he propped up the twelfth stick. This he lighted. When it was smoldering properly, sending off its stream of heavy perfumed smoke, he turned away.

It was just seven-thirty when he lighted the incense.

What a relief that it was all over! So simple! Just this one little detail of planted evidence. That was clever—not to try and make the thing complicated. Just this incense, which would give him a perfect alibi. It was burning nicely; he could see the red dot of fire at the end of the lighted stick. Already the exotic perfume was noticeable.

Milkin was ready. In the outer reception room he stood for a moment examining himself under the light there. No signs of stain upon his linen. He smoothed his coat, his hair, and adjusted his necktie. Lighted a cigarette. Picked up his hat, gloves and cane. Yes, everything was ready. He had left no fingerprints anywhere. His own appearance was perfect. He twirled the waxen ends of his mustache, switched off the reception room light and departed.

It was nearly quarter of eight. Now for Jenks. The door-man should be down there waiting to close up. Milkin composed his face and sauntered nonchalantly down the stairs.

Jenks was there. Milkin slipped him a bill.

"You'd better be getting along, Jenks," he said easily. "I'm sorry to have kept you waiting." He smiled significantly as he added: "Mr. Lentz tells me he has a lady coming—about eight-thirty. A lady—and he has sent me away because he wishes to be alone. You—ah—understand, Jenks? You are discreet?"

The five dollar tip had made Jenks very discreet indeed. He grinned.

"Sure, Mr. Milkin. An' she'll use the night bell?"

"Yes. Mr. Lentz will admit her."

Milkin waited while Jenks closed up. It was a small,

three-story office building just off Broadway in the Forties. Lentz owned it; and the Lentzkin Studio occupied the entire second floor. Only two other tenants, and both had closed for the night. Jenks locked the lower front door, and he and Milkin went down the street toward Broadway. Milkin remarked upon the time. Jenks was part of his alibi; Jenks would remember and swear to the fact that Milkin had come out at a quarter of eight, leaving Lentz alone in the building.

At Broadway Milkin parted from the man with a pleasant good night. Now for Aimé. Her apartment was only three blocks away. She was expecting him at eight o'clock. Well, he would be there, and he would have her with him right through the rest of the evening.

The negro elevator boy of Aimé's apartment house knew Milkin well. As the elevator ascended again Milkin remarked upon the time. The boy would be another witness.

Aimé welcomed Milkin as lovingly as usual. But she knew what had happened; she could read it in his eyes, though she asked him nothing. Lentz was dead. She knew it. Tonight would be the crisis; they would face the police together. And, in a day or so the danger would be all over. The business of the Lentzkin Studio would belong solely to Milkin. The building that housed it would be his.

Lentz was fifty years old, this night that he died. Milkin was twenty-eight. Russians, they had come to America together ten years before. Milkin, then a boy of eighteen, was Lentz's ward. A year ago Lentz had shown Milkin his will. He had no relatives over here—none anywhere. The will gave Milkin everything.

From a paltry five thousand a year—his junior-partner

share of the profits—Milkin now would have the building and the business. Lentz had just turned down an offer of a hundred and fifty thousand for them both. Milkin would accept it. A rich man—no more work—no more business to bother with. Now he would marry Aimé and live a life of luxury and ease.

A stake worth playing for! Aimé knew he was playing for it. And she would stand by him.

Milkin was unusually silent, with all these thoughts surging in his mind. He was waiting for ten o'clock to come; at ten o'clock he would make his next move.

Aimé played the piano for him, and sang. She, too, was waiting. He had told her that Lentz was alone in the studio—that at ten o'clock they would phone Lentz and ask him over for a little supper. Aimé's lips pressed together in a thin scarlet line; and her beautiful face went impassive as the Sphinx.

2

THE HOURS DRAGGED. It was horrible, this waiting. Then at last Milkin went to the 'phone. The hallboy downstairs made the connection. But the Lentzkin Studio did not answer.

Aimé—actress that she was—merely raised her eyebrows. It was a farce, this that she and Milkin were playing. Milkin said steadily:

"I told him I would phone him at ten, to see if he were through his work."

And Aimé said: "Perhaps he's sick. He was not well, he told me yesterday."

Their eyes met; a hush seemed in the room. Milkin was cold as ice inside, but he smiled.

"Suppose we go and see? He should answer the 'phone, Aimé—he said he would be there."

Silently, she got her wraps. A beautiful woman—a woman to be proud of. Milkin's cold fingers lingered on the warmth of her shoulder as he held her cape.

The elevator boy took them down, and Milkin told him where they were going. Soon they would be back with Mr. Lentz.

It was quarter past ten when they let themselves into the dark office building with Milkin's night key. There was a policeman on the nearby corner; Milkin had greeted him as they went past. They went into the building; up the dark stairs; into the reception room. Milkin switched on the light and called:

"Lentz! George—are you here?"

His voice echoed into silence. Aimé now avoided his eyes, as they stood there together. Her face was white under the rouge. They went into the studio. The incense was still burning—a dim point of red in the gloom, and the close air was sickeningly heavy with it.

Milkin discovered the body, lying there on the floor of the dark-room. He called Aimé forward. Agitated. Frightened. He felt that he was acting well. And so was Aimé. Questioning each other—what a farce! Searching the rooms. Phoning for the police; and then rushing downstairs together to get the policeman on the corner. Bringing him up with them; and he knew that they had entered the building no more than a minute or so before.

Together the three of them sat down to wait. The policeman also phoned. Then they waited, touching nothing—everything must be left as it was found. What a terrible thing! Poor Lentz!

And then the authorities came. Several men. One or two in uniform. A fingerprint man with his paraphernalia; and a quiet, grave sort of fellow in plainclothes. His name was Marberry; he appeared to be in charge.

Milkin talked very little. Expressed horror and grief at the death of his friend. Told his story succinctly; and Aimé and the policeman from the corner corroborated him. This Marberry listened silently; then occasionally he darted swift questions. His glance seemed everywhere—gray eyes, masked in an inscrutable face. Milkin was suddenly afraid of those eyes.

THE PRELIMINARY STORY was soon told. Marberry and his men went into the studio and the dark-room. Their examination began. Then other men arrived; one of them was a physician.

Milkin and Aimé sat on the big divan in the studio, watching and listening. Occasionally whispering together. But Milkin said as little as possible. He noted that the incense was still burning; soon this Marberry, if he were clever at all, would make deductions from that incense.

The whole place was now brightly lighted. The men were poking about. A big policeman stood guard at the outer door. The fingerprint man, like a hound on a trail, was nosing everywhere.

Marberry and the physician were in the dark-room examining the body. Milkin could hear them whispering. Then after a time the physician came out, and with a few low words to the policeman, he departed.

But this Marberry—was he so dumb he didn't realize the significance of that incense? Milkin feared he might have to put the detective on the track by mentioning it himself. But he didn't want to do that.

Marberry had been working now for some time with another man in the dark-room. The other man came out and went away. What was Marberry doing in there? It terrified Milkin—not knowing what was going on.

The detective came out at last. He went to the incense which was still burning. And he consulted his watch. Milkin's heart leaped with triumph. He heard himself say surprisingly: "If you could only determine when that was lighted—" He stopped, and cursed himself for having blurted out a thing like that.

Marberry turned around. "Yes, that's just what I was thinking."

Milkin breathed again. It had passed all right. But he must be more careful—say nothing, absolutely nothing. And then abruptly he noticed that Marberry had evidently been examining the incense before. Someone had placed a square of white paper on the table under it.

Marberry came over and sat down before Milkin and Aimé. He seemed waiting for something; he said something about waiting for the return of a man he had sent away. And, while waiting, he now chatted pleasantly, rehearsing the facts. Aimé was a good witness. She was calm and convincing. She smiled in quiet, friendly fashion at the detective.

"Wait," Marberry interrupted once. "You can prove that you were here with Lentz alone from seven o'clock until quarter of eight. I understand that. And also that you weren't here again until you came about quarter past ten and discovered the body. It's obvious then that the murder was committed between eight and ten?"

"Of course," said Milkin. He felt like smiling triumphantly, but he did not; he merely looked sober and earnest.

Marberry went on: "Did you develop any plates during that time you were here with Lentz?"

Milkin shook his head.

"Did Lentz?"

"No."

"You're sure of that?"

Of course Milkin was sure of it. "George was going

to develop them later. And this woman coming here to see him at half-past eight." Milkin had already told that Lentz was expecting a visitor. Some unknown woman. The Lentzkin Studio had many beautiful stage women among its clients. Milkin meant the implication to be that this one had killed Lentz. Lentz had a reputation with women; what more reasonable than that one of them had done this?

Marberry said quietly: "Yes, I know. And when you were here alone with Lentz you didn't either of you go into the dark-room?"

"No," reiterated Milkin. "We were talking, out here in the studio."

Marberry's glance went to the incense. "Did you light that while you were here from seven fifteen to eight o'clock?"

Milkin's heart thumped. "No," he said.

"Did Lentz light it during that time?"

"No."

"It wasn't burning when you left?"

"No," Milkin repeated. "Men do not burn incense. It is for—"

"Women," smiled Marberry. "Well, I believe you're right."

Relief flooded over Milkin. Marberry was clever after all. Not too clever—just clever enough. Marberry was figuring it out, just the way Milkin expected he would. Some woman had arrived, probably between eight thirty and nine o'clock. Lentz, for the meeting, had lighted the incense just before she came. Marberry added:

"You see, I have a way of computing when that incense was lighted. Those sticks originally are ten inches long.

Eleven of them of that length are lying there. The twelfth has burned down several inches. I've been timing the rate at which it burns. Assuming it was its full length when it was lighted—then it was lighted at quarter of nine. If it was an old stick which had been lighted before—then Lentz or the woman must have lighted it later than quarter of nine."

Milkin glowed with triumph, but on his face was a look of mild interest. He had fooled this detective. These incense sticks were of an unusual type—Milkin had searched the Oriental shops carefully to find them. Marberry had never seen any like them before. The detective was assuming now that their original length was ten inches—because these eleven unused ones were that length.

But the sticks had originally been *twelve inches long*. Milkin had carefully shortened these eleven. The twelfth stick which he had lighted—at half-past seven—had been its full twelve inches. Milkin had experimented with all this days before. It worked out perfectly; it had fooled this detective. It proved—to this detective at any rate—that someone had been here in the studio at quarter of nine or later—at which time he had been with Aimé.

All this Milkin told himself was triumph. His plans had been clever; they were working out beautifully.

3

THEN MARBERRY'S MAN returned. He seemed to have brought with him some bottles of chemicals. And some kind of an optical instrument. What the devil? He and Marberry started for the dark-room. Marberry stopped before the incense. His body kept Milkin from seeing clearly. Then he saw that the detective had removed the sheet of paper which had been placed there.

The assistant stopped before Milkin. "Have you got a pair of scales? A delicate balance?"

What the devil? "Yes," Milkin said. "They are in the dark-room."

Marberry was saying to someone: "The woman murdered him just as he was starting to develop a plate. The plate-holder fell from his hands. It was lying on the floor beside the body. Evidently she waited until she got him in the dark-room, so she could sneak up behind him."

Milkin remembered that that was just what had happened—they were figuring it all out right, except the time of the murder, and the murderer! He smiled to himself.

Presently Marberry and the man who had arrived with the bottles went into the dark-room.

Another interval of waiting. What were they doing in there? Milkin could hear the murmurs of their low-toned conversation; the rattle of bottles and trays. A long, oppressive time of waiting. The policeman still stood silent guard over the outer doorway. Reporters had come and been sent away; some were loitering out there now.

It was well past midnight. He and Aimé whispered occasionally. What was all this? An unreasoning fear was surging within Milkin. Then suddenly the dark-room door opened. Marberry and his assistant came out. Marberry said:

"As we thought, Lubin. The ashes from that stick of incense all fell to the table beneath it. The original length of the stick was not determinable—merely because the others were ten inches long did not influence us. But the ashes proved a great deal. We weighed the ashes which that stick yielded in half an hour's burning, and we weighed the total of all its ashes. Easy enough to compute that it has been burning since about half-past seven!"

He whirled on Milkin. "You were here at that time! It's queer that you should have stated so positively that the incense was *not* burning!"

Milkin felt the blood draining from his face, but he fought to hold himself firm. "Why—why, I didn't—" Stammering, but then he conquered it. "I didn't light it. Possibly Lentz did—I didn't see him do it. I'm sorry if I misinformed you by being so positive."

Marberry's searching gaze turned away. Milkin was cold, shivering inwardly. The evidence of the incense which he had planned so carefully had fallen through. Why had he not thought of those cursed ashes? He tried to bolster up his faltering courage. The incense had been a link in his own alibi, but he would have to get along without it. Suppose it *had* been lighted at half-past seven? What of it?

They'd have to prove that the murder was committed about that time—and that they could never do. Milkin was frightened, but, above everything, he knew he must not show it. As though through the cloud of his tumultuous thoughts he heard Marberry's voice:

"It was well after eleven o'clock when Dr. Franks examined the body. He could not tell the time of the death close enough to give us the proof we needed. But the dark-room gave us some interesting theories. Lentz was murdered just as he started to develop a plate. The slide was half drawn."

What was the man getting at? Milkin strove to keep his face impassive. Was Aimé frightened? He did not dare look at her. Marberry's voice went on, still calmly addressing his associate: "To place the time of this murder was vital, Lubin." He whirled around suddenly upon Milkin. "*You'll* be interested in this! Ruby light, as you know, carries only very weak actinic rays—the rays which affect photographic plates. But in the hours during which half of that plate lay exposed to that ruby light those rays did affect it somewhat. We developed it—and found those parts of its lower half which should have been clear were fogged to a certain shade of gray!"

Milkin heard himself stammering: "Oh! Why—yes, that's interesting!"

"Yes, isn't it?" The detective's tone was sardonic. And now it was openly menacing. "Well, with a measurement of the actinic power of that particular ruby light—and a few simple chemical reactions—you understand, Milkin— with chloride of gold and oxalic acid, for instance, to make certain of it—we learned just what that light would do in the way of fogging that brand of plate.

"All simple enough. And a perfect timepiece, Milkin! The result gave us the exact number of minutes it took that ruby light to fog that plate as it did! The murder, Milkin, was committed at seven-fifteen, or very close to it—and you admit and you have proof that you were here alone with Lentz at that time!"

The words blurred in Milkin's ears. His head was roaring. Dimly, in all that swaying scene, he saw figures advancing upon him—felt hands gripping him.

A BAR OF POISONED LICORICE

"A CASE, GENTLEMEN, of attempted murder," said the Doctor. "Most of you have heard, no doubt, of Jonathan J. Blake, octogenarian philanthropist. Someone of his family has attempted to murder him."

"I shouldn't say we could be certain of that," the Lawyer interposed.

"No, but it is fairly obvious." The Doctor gazed at the group of men gathered in the private clubroom. "The idea, gentlemen, is this: Mr. Blake narrowly escaped taking poison. It may have been an accident; or it may have been a deliberate attempt by one of his household. There is no evidence, except the poison itself. We felt that to give the matter to the police would avail nothing, and I suggested that perhaps we of the Scientific Club could handle it by our different method. There may have been no attempted crime at all, in which case no harm will have been done by our experiment. Mr. Blake said nothing to his family; he told only myself, his physician."

The Banker said, "Give us the details, Frank."

"I will," agreed the Doctor. "Briefly, then: Jonathan J. Blake is now eighty-two years old. Hale and hearty—a man who might conceivably have another ten years of life remaining. A bachelor—a very wealthy man, and all his heirs chance to be members of his present household.

Call that the motive, if you like—a desire to hasten the inheritance. The motive is immaterial; as I say, there is no evidence. This will be merely a question of fact—our attempt to identify the criminal, if there is one, and obtain a confession.

"Mr. Blake has given freely to charity, but there remains an estate of several million dollars, all of which he has divided among five people. He is a curious old man. Kindly at heart, but very dogmatic. Difficult, I'm sure, to live with. He rules his household with a rod of iron. He lives unpretentiously—almost plainly. He has an obsession that it is wrong to spend money for luxuries—he keeps his family upon a basis of strict economy. And he is always looking for worthy charities to which he can donate, so that his wealth is steadily dwindling."

The Chemist said dryly, "I can understand why the heirs would have a motive."

"Quite so. Well, as I was saying—"

"Let's get down to it, Frank," the Banker interrupted. "Who are the heirs? Are you going to have them, here tonight?"

"Yes. Mr. Blake is bringing them." The Doctor glanced at his watch. "He said they would be here punctually at nine o'clock. I will be brief. Twenty years ago, Jonathan Blake adopted a boy and girl—twins. They are twenty-five years old now—George and Anna. The boy is inclined to be wild and postpones going to work; and the girl has recently shown a predilection for the handsome family chauffeur. I give you Blake's version of it—but aside from that I imagine his adopted children are decent enough.

"Of the household there is, besides the twins, the chauf-

*"But gentlemen, he wanted that bit of incriminating evidence—
wanted it so that he might destroy it—or perhaps he was
fearful now that someone else might eat it. And that first
minute, there with the others in the room, he was planning
how he might get it.... Miss Anna, who followed him, missed
the licorice bar which she remembered seeing at the first
observation. She asked Dr. Gregg about it, but he silenced her.
It's obvious isn't it? The criminal stole that bar of licorice—
there wasn't any place in the room to hide it—no way of
getting rid of it—probably he's got it in his pocket now."*

feur, Robert Thorpe; the secretary, one William Fontaine, a
man about thirty-five; and the middle-aged housekeeper,
Mrs. Green. Thus, five of them, gentlemen, any one of
whom had opportunity and motive for the crime. The
housekeeper, chauffeur and secretary are all of some years'
service. All know the terms of Mr. Blake's will—the bulk
of his estate divided equally between the twins, but very
handsome legacies for each of the other three.

"The circumstances are these: I must tell you first—
though Mr. Blake is perfectly well—compatible with his
advanced years—he is always experimenting with reme-

dies to improve his physical condition. So long as they are harmless, I have let him go ahead." The Doctor smiled. "Perhaps I couldn't stop him anyway—he's very eccentric—and very obstinate. At any rate, he nibbles often at soda mints; or little peppermint sticks. He chews pepsin gum inordinately; and lately he has taken to nibbling at licorice bars. A variety of such things, and a few of the milder household drugs. He keeps them all in his bathroom medicine cabinet—to which anyone of the household has easy access.

"A week ago he took a bite from a new bar of licorice. He thought it tasted peculiarly—at all events he didn't eat it. Then he seemed to remember that of the bar he had last replaced in the cabinet, he had sucked on one end. This one did not show that. He said nothing of his suspicions, but at once brought the licorice to me. I have had it analyzed. It contains a deadly poison, gentlemen. Enough in one little bite, to have killed him!"

Before the Doctor could continue, the door opened and an attendant announced, "Mr. Jonathan J. Blake and party to see Dr. Adams."

"Bring them up," the Doctor ordered. "Gentlemen, those are all the facts—all the evidence we have. It will not take long—if we can find this criminal at all. You just say nothing—just listen and watch…. Are you all ready, Jack?"

"Yes," said the Very Young Man nervously. "Everything's all ready. Dr. Gregg has the paper and pencils—and I've got the stuff all ready in the other room."

The Doctor nodded, and turned to the Alienist. "Dr. Gregg, as you advised, we'll take them all into the other room together at first. Give them—say sixty seconds?"

"Yes," agreed the Alienist. "That's long enough."

"And then—sixty seconds each, as they go in singly? You keep the time, Jack—but don't even go into the room, except at first when they are all there together. Be with them then—watch them closely."

The hall door opened; Jonathan J. Blake and the five members of his family were ushered in. The room was in confusion for a moment as the Doctor introduced them to the club members. The twins sat together on a leather settee. They were a good-looking youth and girl—this George and Anna Blake; but plainly not of the patrician blood of their foster father. Old Blake was obviously an aristocrat to his fingertips—a stern, fine old face surmounted by a shock of snow-white hair.

Robert Thorpe, the chauffeur, was a muscular, handsome man of about thirty. He drew his chair close to Anna; began whispering to her. The secretary, William Fontaine, sat apart—a thin, pale-faced man who looked thirty-five or forty. The housekeeper, Mrs. Green, was a middle-aged woman of matronly aspect, dressed in black sateen, in the style of a bygone age. She was plainly flustered by the number of men in the room; she sat on the edge of her chair nervously twisting her fingers. But the others were all seemingly at ease, though plainly curious to know what new eccentricity of old Blake had brought them here. The twins said something to that effect.

"You're all here because I told you to come," Blake exclaimed testily. "I've a purpose, which is not for you to criticize." He had seated himself beside the Doctor; he glared at his household.

The secretary said, in a soft almost effeminate voice, "They meant no offense, Mr. Blake."

The chauffeur said nothing; the housekeeper murmured voluably that she was always ready and willing to do anything she was told; but no one heeded her.

The Doctor said quickly, "I'm sure Mr. Blake doesn't really mind being called eccentric. You of course are all wondering why we asked you here. Call it an eccentricity of Mr. Blake's, if you like." His glance to the old man flung a swift warning, then he smiled and added, "I'm one person you cannot bully, can you, Mr. Blake?… Of course you cannot, and so I'm going to tell them plainly why they are here…. Mr. Blake, my friends, has recently become interested in psychology. Dr. Gregg here is an alienist, as you perhaps know, of national fame. These other gentlemen are all interested in the subject—but they are here merely as spectators.

"In a word, Mr. Blake a week or so ago, suggested that Dr. Gregg put him through the various tests to determine the condition of his mentality. We were surprised; and I know Mr. Blake was gratified to have us tell him that his mental powers, at eighty-two, far surpass the average of any age. Perhaps he is vain about it; at any rate he is eccentric enough to demand that those of his family and household go through the same tests—"

Old man Blake said, "There isn't one of them can make any showing at all."

The Doctor laughed. "Perhaps not, Mr. Blake—though don't be too sure. They may not be as stupid as you think they are."

It put the affair upon a basis of lightness and jocularity,

which was the Doctor's purpose. There was a confusion of questions, explanations and argument. None of the visitors displayed any opposition to the experiment: they seemed not to take it seriously; George Blake declared that he would probably fail ignominiously, but that he was sure Anna was dumber than himself. They were all smiling except Mrs. Green. The housekeeper was plainly frightened; she didn't understand what they were talking about; she was willing to go through with it only out of loyalty to her employer.

The Doctor said, "It won't hurt you, Mrs. Green—I promise you that. The first test is merely to demonstrate accuracy of memory." The smile left his face as he added, "I want you all to pay careful attention. The first is an observation test for memory. In the adjoining room we have a table with a number of small articles on it. They are all articles taken from Mr. Blake's home. Perfectly familiar to you—you have seen them all many times. You are each going in twice to observe the table—all together first, to look at the articles sixty seconds. Then one at a time for another sixty seconds. We will supply you with paper and pencil.... Jack, get them from Dr. Gregg and pass them around.... You are to write from memory when you come out a list of as many of the articles as you can remember. That's simple enough, isn't it?"

It was; and as soon as Mrs. Green had thoroughly understood it, they were ready. The Very Young Man had handed out the slips of paper and lead pencils. The Doctor said:

"You are not to use the paper and pencil while in the room. Understand? But the moment you come out you may start your list. No talking or laughing now. Anyone who makes a comment, or glances at any list besides his own is disqualified. Keep your mind firmly on remembering what you see. If you do that you'll have no time for anything else. Write your name now at the top of your list."

A hush fell upon the room. Silently the Very Young Man led them through the inner doorway. The detective, who had not been introduced and who had been sitting in a secluded corner of the main room, rose and whispered to the Alienist. The adjoining room was about twenty feet square. It had no windows; no other door. It was wholly bare save for a single large table which stood in the center of the room with a shaded electric globe directly over it. The articles on the table were in the full glare of the light, but the room itself was in shadow. There were about two dozen of the articles. A pair of scissors; an ash-tray; a package of cigarettes; a spool of thread; a single needle; a pin; a lead pencil; and six or eight articles from old Blake's medicine cabinet—a bar of licorice; a package of chewing gum; toothpaste; a toothbrush and others. All small articles each in plain sight, ranged in orderly rows.

The five subjects of the experiment gathered about the table, eying its contents. The Very Young Man stood at one end of the table, watch in hand. At the open door, unseen by them all, the detective was peering in, with the Alienist standing beside him.

"Time's up," the Very Young Man announced peremptorily. "All out, please. Hurry, there!"

With a last reluctant look, they filed out—Mrs. Green was muttering to herself; Anna Blake laughed. George Blake said, "I'm mixed up already—can you remember any of 'em, Anna?"

"Stay apart now," commanded the Alienist. "Write down what you remember. Next time you go in I want you to count the total number of articles on the table. Remember that number, and when you come out put it on the top of your list."

There was another short silence—a minute or two—while they started their lists. Every eye in the room was upon them.

"Now," said the Alienist, "you are going in again one by one. Then you can add to your list when you come out.... Be sure now to count the total number of articles and put that number on the top of your list.... Mrs. Green, first. Let me have your pencil and paper please—I'll give it to you when you come out."

The housekeeper handed them over as she passed the Alienist at the doorway. The Very Young Man was there, still with his watch in hand.

"I'll rap on the door in sixty seconds, Mrs. Green. Come out promptly, please."

He closed the door upon her. While she was within the Alienist scanned her partial list, and on a slip of his own made an entry.

The Very Young Man rapped; then opened the door. "Come out, Mrs. Green. Take your list from Dr. Gregg.... Did you count the articles? Good. Write it down.... Who's next?"

"George Blake," called the Alienist.

The performance was repeated with each of them in turn. George Blake; the chauffeur; Anna Blake; and then the secretary. As Anna Blake came out she whispered to Dr. Gregg a question, but he silenced her vehemently. They were presently all in the main room busy with the lists. The Alienist went in to examine the table; when he came out he glanced at the Very Young Man's watch.

"How long, Jack?"

"Time's up now. Did—"

"Sh!"

The Alienist called, "Time's up. Let me have your lists please."

The Very Young Man collected them. At a table apart, the Alienist and the Doctor examined them; and examined the notes the Alienist had made. It only took a moment; but in that moment a suppressed air of excitement had spread about the room. An unnatural, strained silence, which everyone instinctively seemed to avoid breaking. It may have originated with the club members who knew the real import of what was transpiring; and it spread so that abruptly everyone felt the tension. Old man Blake was sitting grim and silent; his face gone pale, his thin lips pressed tightly together, his eyes black and ominous, roaming from one to the other of the suspected members of his household. George Blake regarded him. "What's the matter? What is—"

The Doctor leaped to his feet. "You've a right to know, all of you. And it won't take me a minute to tell you. An attempt was made a few days ago to murder Mr. Blake.... Silence, please.... Yes, this has been more than an innocent psychological test—a psychological test to find a murderer! And we've found him!"

The Doctor turned to address the room in general.... "Gentlemen, as I told you a while ago, one of the members of Mr. Blake's home substituted a poisoned bar of licorice for the one in his bathroom cabinet. This criminal had easy access to it—put it there and waited for Mr. Blake to eat some of it, and die. The criminal was frightened—a guilty person always is, after he has committed a crime. Wondered if Mr. Blake had found out it was poison— haunted by the fear that he would be discovered. But he didn't dare show his fear. Tried to get the licorice bar back again—but it was gone from the cabinet. That frightened him still more. He wanted that incriminating evidence destroyed—he was sorry, perhaps, that he ever attempted murder. And he came here tonight with guilt in his heart.

Mrs. Green's teeth were chattering; the others sat white faced and silent. One of them was guilty but he held himself quiet.

The Doctor went on vehemently, "What I have said of the murderer's feelings, gentlemen, is pure assumption— but it's a very easy guess that I'm right. And we have proof of the crime—and the criminal identified—here in his own writing on his list!

"I'll follow his mental processes. He was suspicious of this test—he thought doubtless we had had the bar of licorice analyzed—as in fact we did—and that this was some scheme to trap him. He was wary. He went into that little room over there with his companions. On the table he saw the bar of licorice. He thought it was the poisoned bar—it looks identically like it. He was relieved. His attempted crime had not yet been discovered, he thought; and the licorice had disappeared from Mr. Blake's cabinet because we had taken it for this innocent test. And his suspicions of our motive were lulled—he forgot to be wary.

"But gentlemen, he wanted that bit of incriminating evidence—wanted it so that he might destroy it—or perhaps he was fearful now that someone else might eat it. And that first minute, there with the others in the room, he was planning how he might get it.

"We were fairly sure then of his identity. When he handed his list to Dr. Gregg—as he went in for the second time—he had only been able to write three articles on it, and one of them was wrongly named. His mind was too busy with his crime for him to think of anything else."

The Doctor took the lists from the Alienist. "The table, gentlemen, held twenty-four articles. These lists, after the first observation, all contained from six to twelve articles correctly named—except the guilty list. That named three—one wrongly. The bar of licorice was the most prominently displayed article on the table. Every list at once bore it—except the guilty one. He didn't dare name it—he had planned what he was going to do. He went back for the second time—counted the articles and put on his list a total count of twenty-three instead of twenty-four. Those who went into the room *ahead of him* counted twenty-four; those who *followed* him counted twenty-three. Miss Anna, who followed him, missed the licorice bar which she remembered seeing at the first observation. She asked Dr. Gregg about it, but he silenced her. It's obvious isn't it? The criminal stole that bar of licorice—there wasn't any place in the room to hide it—no way of getting rid of it—probably he's got it in his pocket now…. Marberry! Hold him!"

The chauffeur was on his feet; the detective leaped for him; with the muscular Very Young Man they overpowered him—found the bar of licorice in his pocket. He confessed.

He was in love with Anna Blake; secretly she had agreed to marry him. They would inherit a fortune, and he wanted it. If they married while Mr. Blake was alive, he knew Anna would be disinherited. His brother worked in the licorice factory; had prepared the poisoned bar upon a promise of later money payment.

He told it freely, brokenly. And ended, "That's all—take me away—arrest me—let's have done with it—I tell you I've been frightened as hell—I'm glad it's over."

For the first time in half an hour old man Blake spoke. "I don't care to prosecute him—have I the right to let him go, Mr. Marberry?"

The detective nodded dubiously.

"Well then—send him away—I'll give him a ticket to the coast—anywhere away from Anna. I guess he's been punished enough by his own guilty conscience.... Anna! Forget him, child—you made a mistake, that's all."

The girl was crying.

WHAT THE TYPEWRITER TOLD

"YOU SAY YOU know who the murderer is?" the Alienist asked.

"No," corrected the Doctor. "I said we know who committed the crime."

The Banker sat up abruptly with a gesture of impatience. "What's the difference? Why split hairs over technicalities? You said—"

"Wait, George." The Doctor gazed around the private clubroom at the little group of members seated before him. "Gentlemen, this case is peculiar. We have proof of the criminal's identity. But the crime itself—the trouble is, we have no determination yet as to what crime was committed."

"The man is dead," the Astronomer observed.

"Quite so. But manslaughter, murder, and most of all premeditated murder, are very different things."

"Very different," the Lawyer commented.

The Doctor added, "More than that, this crime on the surface appears to be only an attempt at blackmail."

"Why not outline the case for us?" the Banker demanded. "These hypothetical discussions—"

"I will," the Doctor agreed. A package lay before him on the table; he drew from it a litter of papers—anonymous typewritten letters, dirty and rumpled most of them; all of them on plain white paper of assorted sizes; and a variety of envelopes, all addressed in typewriting to "L.C. McIlray, 2860 Orange Ave., Maple Grove, New Jersey."

The Doctor spread them out. "The murder letters, gentlemen—I'll read some of them to you. First, the case briefly, is this: Leonard C. McIlray, up to the time of his death two weeks ago, was Advertising Manager of the Tonola Phonograph Company out in Maple Grove. A man of fifty-five, of exceedingly kindly, gentle nature, beloved by his employees. Nine years ago he was left a widower. He had fairly idolized his wife—yet in one short year he married his business secretary—a handsome dark-eyed girl then twenty-six or so. By his first wife he had one child, Alan, who now is twenty-eight. He was assistant to his father—he will now be advertising manager of the company. By this second wife there is one child—a little girl now five years old. Elsie—blue-eyed, golden-haired. Her father worshipped her in inverse ratio to a seeming estrangement which of recent years was growing between himself and his young wife. And there was an estrangement—not outward, not admitted—between him and his son Alan, doubtless because the son did not approve of his father's second marriage."

"If this man got murdered," said the Banker, "I for one would like to hear how it happened."

"You shall, George, but those family details are necessary. McIlray died just after dinner at his home in Maple Grove. I must tell you one thing more. The man was in fair health, but for years his heart had been organically defective. With care—very moderate exercise—the avoidance of any severe digestive disturbance—and most of all the

"These letters shocked Mr. McIlray and caused his death. As you know, the police suspected one of you five as the writer of them—" ... "They suspected you," the Doctor reiterated. "They still do—but their grilling was unavailing, and they had no proof. We of the Scientific Club, however, now have proof! We know now which of you wrote those letters!"

complete absence of excitement of any kind—he could have lived with that heart to his normal span. But gentlemen, understand me, he was in a chronic condition where any shock, any violence physical or mental, would have caused his instant death. And *this was known* freely to his family and his business associates.

"I come now to the murder—if murder it were. The family had just finished dinner. The front doorbell rang. The maid answered it; and it was the postman who handed her a letter for Mr. McIlray. This letter." The Doctor indicated one of the dirty typewritten envelopes before him. "McIlray recognized it doubtless. He did not open it, but suddenly excused himself, left the dining-room with an agitation that was obvious. Later the maid said he had gone to his den—a small room on the lower floor off the hall. Alan went in there after him. He lay on the floor, dead, with a loaded revolver in his hand!”

“Suicide!” exclaimed the Banker.

“Don't be an ass, George. A shot would have been heard. The revolver had not been fired. There was not a mark on his body. He died of heart failure induced by sudden, violent mental shock.”

“What about the letter he had just received?” the Chemist asked.

“It could not at first be found. When the physician came— Gentlemen, now we approach the pathetic aspect of this case. McIlray had been laboring for weeks under a terrible strain—a fear—and he had kept it to himself—had dared tell no one—except his little daughter Elsie. Only the child did he feel he could trust. When the physician arrived the little girl sidled up to him. ‘My daddy said, if he got dead I must tell you to send for the police!’ That was the message from the dead man she gave the family physician.

“Marberry here was called in. When he arrived, the child asked him naïvely if he were the police. And then she told him her daddy had said, ‘Look in the organ.’ An old-fashioned organ stood in a corner of the den. Anticipating a possible death, he had left his secret with the little girl, and faithfully—without knowing the meaning of it all—she had delivered his messages.

“They looked in the organ. Found all these letters, with the last one he had just received crammed in hastily after them. He had evidently kept the revolver secretly about his person—though he was the last man who would use a weapon. And there in the den, he had drawn it, and dropped dead with it in his hand. With the letters Marberry found this little book, his diary." The Doctor produced a small red book. "This and the letters, gentlemen, tell us the whole—or nearly all—the pathetic story. Look here—I'll read you extracts."

ANONYMOUS LETTERS

THE LETTERS WERE all anonymous. Mailed at irregular intervals, they dated back over a period of some five weeks. All of them were posted either in Maple Grove, neighboring towns, or New York City. A series of threatening murder letters. Blackmail—the threat of kidnaping, or killing the child. Then the open threat of murder, the child and himself as well. The Doctor explained them, and then opened the diary. Its early pages were the usual diary record. Then came the date of the first of these letters; and from then on it was the unburdening of his heart toward this sinister thing that had come to him. And all of it he had kept secret. The Doctor said solemnly:

"You have only to read these letters and the diary to know why he kept it secret. Men of sterner nature would have gone to the police at once. But not McIlray. Listen to this—the first letter:

" 'L.C. You don't know me but I know you damn well. You read this letter and then I guess you'll figure on turning it over to the police right away. Well don't you do it, L.C. You burn it and keep it to yourself. If you don't....' "

A rambling letter. The Doctor read it through—a full page of it, single spaced. And the thing carried conviction. It was obvious that the writer knew McIlray almost intimately. The letter told him of things he had said and done which convinced him of that—convinced him that the writer was close to him. And the letter threatened, if he took the affair to the police, or breathed a word of it to any living soul—that his little daughter would be killed. If he spoke to anyone, this enemy would know it—even if members of his own family. And if he took the child away, had her guarded, or made any change in her daily life or his own, it would be known at once and the child would be killed. But if McIlray played fair—donated to the writer a reasonable sum of money to be named later—no harm would come to Elsie.

A series of such letters. And reading them, no one could have doubted their menacing sincerity. A later one specified a thousand dollars, which the father was to bring to a designated place at night. The money was nothing to McIlray compared to even the smallest danger to Elsie.

The diary showed that McIlray had tried to laugh off the first letter. Some crank, fanatic wanting to annoy him. He tried to forget it—but he did not tell the police, or anyone, evidently. Then other letters came. The Doctor read from the diary:

"Whom can I trust? God knows, this could be anyone. It *could* be my wife—my son? But it is not, of course. It could be—one of those I think is a friend. It *must* be one of those. Dare I give this to the police? Of course I must."

But still he did not. A fanatic defied—he recalled having read of many cases where swift death overtook the unfortunate victim who dared fight back. How could he dare take even the slightest chance? He would pay the money asked.

He took the money, alone on foot to the place named. But no one was there to claim it. And the next letter said that the writer had decided a larger amount would be necessary. Five thousand now. But when McIlray obeyed instructions, though the letter said a man would appear to take the money, no one was there.

The Banker demanded, "Why didn't this blackmailer find some safe way of taking the money and go ahead and take it? What object—"

The Doctor waved the question away. "Here is the last letter. 'L. C. Well, so you defied me. That's all right too. But I keep my word—this is the end. I ain't the person to go back on what I say. Well when you get this here note you'll be dead five minutes after. And your kid will be dead in an hour. You can't stop me, and I'll get her too, don't you think I won't. This is the finish.'"

The Doctor said, "But he didn't defy him, gentlemen. McIlray never showed the least defiance."

The Chemist began, "You mean—"

"I mean," returned the Doctor with sudden vehemence, "that the thing is obvious. McIlray's condition was generally known—that for him to suffer any great agitation would be dangerous—that any sudden shock would kill him. This writer knew it, of course. Made no attempt to collect any money. Wrote 'So you've defied me,' just to bring the thing to a climax—to convince McIlray that himself and his little daughter were in immediate deadly danger. The whole thing—a dastardly attempt to murder a man by frightening him to death—and it succeeded."

THE WRITER IDENTIFIED

THERE WAS A momentary silence in the clubroom when the Doctor paused. "There's the whole story, gentlemen. Naturally the first thing was to identify the writer of the letters. Marberry could not. A questioning of McIlray's family and intimates—there are not so many of them who could have written the intimate details these letters contain—ordinary questioning brought nothing.

"But Mr. Manton here—"The Doctor gestured toward one of the club members—"Mr. Manton has made a hobby of typewriting—or I should say a science of it. He has given us absolute proof of who wrote those letters—"

The Doctor raised his hand to check half a dozen eager questions. "Wait, gentlemen! In a moment you shall hear how we got that proof. But here is the point: To identify the letter-writer does not prove premeditated murder. Or murder at all. The criminal may very well say, 'Why all I wanted to do was get some money out of him.' We must prove the *intent to kill*. And this case is unique because the murderer did nothing which in itself could prove his intent. You get the point? Nobody can say from those letters—as a matter of cold legal proof—what was in the writer's mind when he wrote then. His actual planned intent to accomplish what actually occurred, is necessary—his planned intent to frighten McIlray to death—that is what we must prove."

"You can't prove it," the Lawyer exclaimed. "Unless you can get a confession."

The Doctor smiled. "I'm having several of these people brought here tonight—they should be here by now. The criminal is among them—he does not yet know that we have any proof against him. That's why I included others whom he might think we suspected…. Gentlemen, understand me. You'll see presently that this blackmailer-murderer—is what they call hard-boiled. And by his appearance you would never suspect it. A queer character—emotionless—or at least impervious to any emotion which we could induce in him to make him betray himself. Marberry has studied him. We know we cannot make him confess—unless we confront him with positive, irrefutable proof. Then, if we have judged him rightly, he'll confess quite calmly."

"But the proof?" demanded the Lawyer. "How can you prove the intent in his mind? Nobody knows what was in his mind except himself."

"We can prove it," the Doctor said. "You'll see. Now the way Mr. Manton identified who wrote the letters is—"

The Banker interrupted. "Who did write them? If he intended murder not blackmail, what was his motive?"

Before the Doctor could answer the door opened and an attendant announced, "They are all here now, Dr. Adams. Shall I bring them up?"

The Doctor nodded. As the door closed he added briskly,

"You gentlemen are to do nothing except sit quiet and listen.... You have the evidence, Marberry?"

The detective answered that he had. "Good," said the Doctor. "Well, gentlemen, you'll hear in a moment how we identified this letter-writer, for I'm going to explain it to him bluntly. His motive—we have guessed it—and I believe we can now drag it forth. With you as witnesses— the unusualness of this hearing—I think we can get proof of the motive. Not from this hard-boiled murderer— from someone else more susceptible to surprise. That will strengthen our case. And then for our final proof of premeditation—"

THE INQUEST

HE GOT NO further for the door opened and the visitors entered. The murder letters lay scattered on the table, but the Doctor made no move to gather them up. Four men and a woman advanced into the room. They were introduced to the club members, the Doctor making brief frank explanation to his fellow scientists regarding each of them.

The woman was Sibyl McIlray, wife of the dead man. A tall, slim woman of thirty-two, fashionably dressed, with her luxuriant chestnut hair coiled on her head. A stunning woman—in her own estimation—and to do her justice, in the estimation of almost everyone else. Her manner was friendly, though reserved; but there was in it now as she acknowledged the introductions, a hint of patronage, almost of snobbery.

Taking his seat near her, though he seemed to ignore her with the suggestion that a secret animosity might have been between them, was Alan McIlray, the dead man's son by his first wife. A good-looking young man of the promising business type. Of four years service in the Tonola Company, in spite of his youth it seemed likely he would be raised to his father's position.

Beside Alan, sat Raymond Worthington. He was editor

of one of the Tonola House Organs, occasional ad. writer, and general proof reader of the mass of printing the Advertising Department issued. A slim, Byronic-looking man— poetic with his pale skin, dark eyes and longish, wavy black hair.

Next was Frank Boyce, copy writer and all-around man of the Advertising Department. A man of about thirty-five. Solidly-built, with a smooth-shaven, ruddy face, pale eyes, sandy hair and a bald spot. He seemed to smile overmuch; an air of geniality, of which doubtless he was proud, radiated from him.

And last, John Haynes, who kept the records of the voice trials, and wrote for the Advertising Department all its copy of an artistic musical angle. A small man, with a red-brown skin, dark eyes, a rather flat, broad nose, and sleek, oily very straight black hair. A likable fellow, this Haynes—he was well liked in the Tonola Company. Some said he was half American Indian, or of native West Indian descent. Mrs. McIlray considered him a negro.

Such were the visitors, one of whom, the Doctor had said, was this murderous criminal. To the listening club members, it was obvious that all these suspects used typewriters in their daily routine. Except Mrs. McIlray, and she had been a stenographer. She had not given it up, but as a point of fact, had now in her home a small portable machine upon which she typed her social correspondence.

When the visitors were seated, Sibyl McIlray, in a voice cool, gracious, but with annoyance undisguised, demanded abruptly:

"May I ask, Dr. Adams, what your purpose is in this? So—public a gathering—my time is limited—"

Her glance was on the letters lying on the table. Each of the visitors had glanced at them, recognized them from times of various police questionings.

The Doctor answered smilingly. "I asked you all here for an informal unofficial inquiry into the death of Mr. McIlray, as you know. I shall be brief—blunt—even hasty, you may be sure." He paused an instant, and then plunged at once into the heart of his attack.

"These letters—" He gestured toward them—"shocked Mr. McIlray and caused his death. As you know, the police suspected one of you five as the writer of them—" They received it quietly. Not one of them moved, or spoke. Mrs. McIlray raised her pencilled eyebrows and smiled superciliously. "They suspected you," the Doctor reiterated. "They still do—but their grilling was unavailing, and they had no proof. We of the Scientific Club, however, now have proof! We know now which of you wrote those letters!' "

THE PROOF

IT STRUCK THEM like a bomb, surprised, startled them. Yet the keenly watching club members could detect only the normal startled aspect, not the woman, nor anyone of the four men showed guilt. Frank Boyce ejaculated, "By Jove, this is interesting"; and smiled his genial smile. It was out of place; so much so that Alan McIlray, himself very sober, leaned over and audibly whispered, "Shut up, you fool!"

The Doctor went calmly on. "We know which of you wrote those letters. I'm going to tell you how we know.... Mr. Marberry, close that door, please."

The detective closed the only door to the room, locked it ostentatiously and dropped the key in his pocket. He said grimly, and with a faint ironic smile, "Those windows—remember we are nine stories above the street. This guilty person will do well to sit quiet. We ask no confession."

Haynes the Indian, with expressionless impassive face, murmured, "Is one of us supposed to leap through a window? I think this is going to be what they call the third degree."

"You're mistaken," said the Doctor. "I'm not going to question any of you. We have all the proof we need.... I'll continue. The problem, briefly, was this: We had a series of anonymous, typewritten letters, attempting blackmail, threatening murder. We had five suspects, all of whom use typewriters daily—all of whom had the knowledge, the intimate facts concerning Mr. McIlray which would have enabled them to write the letters. Which one—if indeed any of them—was the letter-writer? Mr. Manton here, found out. Let me tell you how."

Raymond Worthington said abruptly, "Why don't you accuse one of us at once? It would save the rest of us from a good deal of apprehension."

"I shall conduct this as I choose," retorted the Doctor with a frown.

Worthington smiled. "Excuse me. I merely implied that you might make an error—accuse the wrong one. Those of us who are innocent naturally are apprehensive."

"There will be no error," said the Doctor.… "An examination of the letters, gentlemen, showed that they were all written by the same person and upon the same machine. Tricks of phraseology, when analyzed, showed but one author. Mr. Manton determined also that the illiteracy of the letters probably was assumed. That was fairly easy to see. Illiteracy is hard to simulate. You have only to examine some real specimens of illiterate letters to see that these are false. The writer then, we reasoned, was a person of education.

"Next, that all were written upon one machine—that too was simple. Typewriters differ—even those of identical make—and more especially after they have become old. Pica type, elite type—different types and different ribbons. Also less blatant differences—some which you cannot notice without a magnifying glass. Letters out of alignment—or a corner of the letters chipped off. These blackmail, murder notes all show the same machine peculiarities—so we know that they were all written upon the same machine—a rather old, decrepit one.

"Now, of course, had this criminal been such a fool as to use his own machine at the office, we could have identified him by that. But he did not. He had some hidden machine, naturally, and since we had no way of finding it, the peculiarities inherent to the typewriter did us no good.... I'd prefer that none of you interrupted me, if you please. I'll be through in a moment."

Frank Boyce had started to speak. The Doctor now wholly ignored the visitors, addressing himself to the club members. "You gentlemen will realize that the differing work done by different typewriters is the same as with different pens in handwriting. In each case—the pen, the machine—they are merely the tools. A stub pen writes a broad stroke; other pens write quite different strokes. Some old pens scratch; some stick in the paper on the ascending stroke. All are mere peculiarities of the tool being used.

"But gentlemen, you all know that in handwriting we do not identify the writer by the pen he used, but by the personal characteristics of his writing. So it is with typewriting! Not so generally known. This criminal did not know it. He considered his machine, but not his typewriting. We have handwriting experts. Mr. Manton here—shall we call him a typewriting expert? He has made a study, a science of it."

The Doctor's words were creating a sensation. But nevertheless, not one of the five visitors showed guilt.

The woman was visibly excited. Three of the men were tense, with what even to one innocent, might have been a normal apprehension; but the Indian still was impassive. The Doctor had said that this criminal was hard-boiled. It seemed so indeed.

"The science of identifying typewriting," the Doctor continued, "I believe will develop into great importance in criminology—and hitherto it has been neglected. I won't weary you with details—here are, briefly, its fundamentals—to give you an idea of what I mean. In studying the work of different typists, we have good work, poor work, erasures, x-ing out letters and words. Those are general characteristics such as of a good or a poor penman—but they are not specifically individual. However, in addition, inherent to all the typing a person does, is an individuality quite comparable though of course not so obvious to the untrained eye, as handwriting. Some of the individualities can be seen at a glance, others only by scrutiny under a magnifying glass. But they are always there.

"Here are some of them. A typist may obviously use the professional touch system, but the stroke will be rather weak with the fourth finger of each of the hands. Most generally that finger, for the ligament tying it gives it less freedom of action than any of the others. The weak stroke, however, might be any finger. Whichever it is, it remains always the same—and since, with the touch system each finger has its allotted letters to strike, the peculiarity can be identified. Under a magnifying glass the least difference of power in the stroke can be discerned.

"Or again. A typist may have an offending finger; and, when making a very light letter, will frequently back space and strike the letter over again. That is readily noticed. Or, an inexpert typist will use the 'hunt and peck,' involving but two fingers at the most of each hand. Such a typist may only use the left hand shift key, and needing a capital letter at the left of the keyboard, will reach over with his right hand and give it a strong poke with his forefinger. Easily seen and recognized."

Frank Boyce, with the grace this time not to smile, murmured, "I wonder which one of us does these things."

The Doctor ignored him. "Another will thump his period unduly hard. A rapid typist again, sometimes goes too fast for his machine. The simple combination of t-h-e—his impetuosity will cause him to strike the t-h so rapidly as to run them inordinately close together—the escapement not quite keeping pace with him.

"Or sometimes, with the combination of a comma followed by a space, a typist of unprofessional training will develop a peculiar ultra-rapid touch, using the right forefinger and the thumb. Even a machine in very good shape will frequently jump two spaces when that is done. A typist prone to that peculiarity will in a single page have that happen several times, yet another typist, using the same machine, would never have it happen.

"You follow me, gentlemen? I might go on with these individualities for a long time—Mr. Manton has tabu-lated nearly a hundred. But I think I've given you enough to show you what we mean. It is true that a typist with extreme care, could disguise or correct many of these pecu-liarities. The two-space jump, for instance, could readily be watched and avoided. But this anonymous letter writer had no such thought. And he was absorbed with the difficulty of simulating illiteracy. Content that he was using a secret machine, he typed in quite his normal fashion.

"Another point. A single sentence of typewriting gives nothing conclusive. It is the average over a large number of sentences. Fortunately in this case, the anonymous letters give us ample length. And you will realize, of course, that for comparison, we had no difficulty in securing from the Tonola office voluminous specimens of typewriting of these four men."

THE ACCUSATION

THE DOCTOR'S TONE turned suddenly grim and menacing. "Gentlemen, there is absolutely no possibility of error. So obvious a result that any twelve jurors will see it at a glance. Each and every one of these anonymous letters—how many peculiarities, Mr. Manton?"

"Nine," responded Manton quietly. "I have tabulated them, marked them in the original anonymous letters."

"Quite so. Nine, gentlemen, no more, no less. Nine—always the same nine in each of the murder notes. We then take the office specimens—the work of four different typists. All have peculiarities—some the same peculiarities in common. But only one of these four typists has that exact set of nine, and *he has them*. That exact set of nine—no more, no less. Is there any room for doubt, gentlemen? The evidence is here, irrevocably typed, mathematically beyond any coincidental possibility."

Manton, at a signal from the Doctor, had produced a sheaf of yellow typewritten pages, office copy of ads, House Organ editorials, articles on the merits of the phonograph, and the like. Pages marked with Manton's penciled notes. And a tabulated list of explanations appended.

The club members leaned forward. Several of the visitors

were on their feet. All recognized the authorship of this office copy. Alan McIlray leaped forward. With this assailant of his father now exposed, the son's wrath played forth.

"You damned murderer. They got you. Got you—"

He was bending over Raymond Worthington; would have attacked him but the detective forced him away. Worthington kept his seat. His face was paler than usual. Sweat was on his forehead, but he forced a smile.

"Murderer?" His voice was calmly, cynically questioning. There was a tremor in it, but it did not break. "Murderer? As I understand it these letters attempt to blackmail. They make idle threats, nothing else. I see no evidence of murder."

The detective was back upon him. "You admit the authorship?"

The Doctor interposed, "He doesn't have to. We've proven it against him. Let him alone—it will go harder with him if he maintains innocence in the face of this evidence."

There was a brief pause, then Worthington made a gesture. "I'm not a fool. I wrote the letters, yes." He had better control of himself now. One of those usual characters whose looks wholly belie their nature. One would have said this long-haired poetic-looking Worthington would have been emotional in the extreme. Yet he was not; was indeed, coolly calculating; his mind now, undoubtedly busy, deciding upon the course to give him the best standing possible with the law he soon would have to face.

"I wrote them," he reiterated. "Make the most of it. My intention was to get some money out of him. He paid me too little in the office." He simulated a momentary vehemence. "I knew he was in delicate health, but forgot it. My God, if I'd realized the letters might shock him—might jeopardize his life—even so, my conscience is clear as to that. I only wanted money. I didn't get it, but I'll admit I tried to."

"We sympathize with you," said the Doctor ironically. "Gentlemen, this fellow knows what he is doing—he's calculating every word. He murdered Leonard McIlray— premeditated murder—and he thinks we cannot prove it. He has had experience with the law—been sentenced twice in England for forgery and petty thievery. You didn't know we were aware of that, did you, Worthington?"

"No," he said calmly. "But since it's a matter of record, I admit it freely."

The Doctor turned away, swinging abruptly to Mrs. McIlray. The woman, to one watching her closely, had been acting very strangely. One might have thought, with this assailant of her dead husband at last unmasked, she would have been triumphant, wrathful of him as was her stepson Alan. Instead she was obviously frightened, apprehensive, with a fear not for herself, but for this Worthington, now trapped and in the hands of the law. At his admission of guilt, "Raymond," in agonized cry had burst from her. The Doctor, who had been observing her more closely than he had the man, now swiftly confronted her, his manner menacing, his voice grim with an edge of steel.

"You know why he did this thing. His motive—you supplied it."

She looked up to him; the color faded from her cheeks, leaving them grotesque with their vivid rouge. His gaze held her as he went on.

"This Worthington is in love with you. You knew it; you reciprocate it—admitted to him your love."

She stammered, "I—why he—"Then resolutely stopped.

"Your friends suspected it," the Doctor went on. "Since we proved this fellow the letter writer, Marberry has quietly been questioning them."

The detective jumped forward, confronted her. "Yesterday you very nearly told me so yourself. You tried to hide it, but you're guilty—I knew it yesterday—guilty as hell."

They would not give her time to speak. The Doctor put in, "Your little daughter Elsie knew it. There's where we got the real information. Knew it, without knowing, thank heaven, what it meant. She told us—told me she overheard you and Worthington. Heard him ask, 'If you were free, Sibyl, would you marry me?' And you said, 'Yes, yes, Raymond, I would.'"

THE MOTIVE

THE DOCTOR SWUNG away. "There is the murder motive, gentlemen. This woman, inheriting the bulk of her husband's estate, would be at his death comparatively rich. Technically a virtuous wife, but she loved this cad—admitted to him that if she were free she would marry him. Sealed—unwittingly her husband's death warrant."

The detective exclaimed: "Elsie heard you say that. You did say it, didn't you? Do you dare deny it?"

She was confused; on the verge of sobbing. "You—you mean—" she half whispered. "You mean, I tried to kill my husband. That's not—"

"Of course not," the Doctor interrupted. "I said the contrary. You could not—or did not—know what this Worthington would do. But you admitted you loved him? Told him—if you were free—you would marry him? We do not blame you—no blame—you meant nothing—"

She broke down. "I mean nothing—that's true. But I did love him—not my husband. That's true. It's all true, what you say."

"Sibyl!" It was a cry of angry warning from Worthington, but she was sobbing and too overwrought to heed it. "I meant nothing wrong—before God, I meant—and I did nothing wrong. I—I could not help loving him. And I told him so—but I told him I'd never divorce Leonard. He was good to me. Good to me, and now he's dead."

The Doctor left her. She was sobbing uncontrolled; and Alan McIlray led her aside, with obvious revulsion yet man enough to comfort her.

The Doctor again fronted Worthington. "So you see, we now have your motive for premeditated murder."

Worthington was gripping the arms of his chair. His eyes roved the room as though instinctively he sought escape. Then they fastened upon the Doctor's face. He sneered.

"The woman's a fool."

"She was, but she isn't any longer."

"You think you could make anyone believe that hysterical story?" He was forcing an argumentative tone, striving to appear at ease.

The Doctor responded calmly, "Of course, and they'll believe the child and the corroborative evidence of everyone who knew you and her."

Worthington's gesture was resigned. "Have it your own way. Say I had a motive. That proves no crime. I swear I intended nothing but blackmail by those letters. You can't prove what was in my mind. I know, and you don't."

"Oh, yes I do. And I can prove it. I will—here and now—mark you, gentlemen—as soon as we knew this Worthington was the criminal we set about finding his hidden typewriter upon which he wrote the notes. He has never been near it since he wrote the last one on the morning of McIlray's death. Naturally he would stay away from it. But to trace his former movements and find it was a simple though laborious piece of detective work. The murder notes were mailed in several towns adjacent to Maple Grove, some in Maple Grove and some here in New York. That last one postmarked noon, was posted in Rollinsdale. It is a fifteen minute trolley ride from Maple Grove; the trolley passes the Tonola factory.

"Marberry found by inquiry, that Worthington left the office about ten-thirty that morning. He has no automobile; and he was observed to take the trolley. It is a branch line; it goes nowhere but to Rollinsdale. From ten-thirty until noon—only an hour and a half—Marberry assumed that Worthington might have gone to his secret typewriter, written and mailed the letter. Mailed it hastily near at hand, near noon and this would, by Worthington's calculations, deliver it in the Maple Grove late afternoon delivery.

"Merely presumptive reasoning on Marberry's part—that the typewriter was in Rollinsdale—but it proved to be correct. The rest was easy. Worthington, most naturally, had hired a room or small office somewhere in Rollinsdale. Probably under an assumed name. But Worthington is a distinctive type—easy to describe, and Rollinsdale is a small place. Marberry, accompanied by myself with two other assistants and Mr. Manton, made a canvass. We found in a cheap boarding house that a man named Blaine, who answered Worthington's description, was renting a room, not sleeping in it, but occasionally using a typewriter. He had said he was an author.

"We found the typewriter, took possession of it. We have it here—an old, battered machine. It has a broken letter which appears in all the murder notes. Additional, clinching evidence. Does this interest you, Worthington?

"Very," he replied, with a faint touch of sarcasm. But his face was even paler than before. The sense that he was trapped must have been coming to him. He added cautiously: "You say you have the machine here? May I see it?"

The Doctor nodded. Marberry had already crossed the room, opened a closet, returning with an old, somewhat dilapidated typewriter, which he placed on the table. Worthington regarded it without emotion; then he gave a mirthless laugh.

"That's the one I used. That landlady will of course identify me and the machine, so I admit it, naturally. But, Doctor Adams, this is all to no purpose. I wrote the letters intending blackmail, nothing more."

"We'll see about that," said the Doctor grimly. A tenseness came to his voice; and it spread, this tenseness, about the room as though his hearers realized that now he had come to the climax of his attack.

"Gentlemen, the vital point now is—did Worthington write these letters merely for blackmail, or with *intent to kill.* We have established that he had a strong motive to desire McIlray's death. But that proves nothing. Did he have in his mind as he wrote, a definite intent to kill? Gentlemen, look at that typewriter, notice it has a nice new black ribbon on it—not the ribbon which was used for the murder notes. That ribbon tells the story! It has been used only once—part of it not at all."

The Doctor pointed to the typewriter which stood now on the table with the electrolier shining full upon it. "On that ribbon, gentlemen, you will find the impressions made by typing upon it just once. A short note—so short that there was no occasion to reverse the movement of the ribbon. The letters are quite legible. Like a sheet of carbon paper used but once, or a new blotter used once, it contains the letters, words, sentences which were impressed upon it."

The Doctor was talking very rapidly now. Worthington had risen to his feet and then had sunk back to his chair.

"Mr. Manton and I very carefully transcribed those words. They were written *previous to Mr. McIlray's death;* remember that. We have positive evidence that Worthington never again returned to the typewriter after that morning. The ribbon shows us a letter to his darling Sibyl. He wrote it; we found in it that same set of his individual peculiarities. A love letter, which he wanted to look nice with a new ribbon, and it states that now that *her husband is dead,* soon she will be his. A foolish letter to write. Doubtless he concluded so and never sent it. But he wrote it, *before his victim died.* That almost proves intent to kill—perhaps not quite. But, gentlemen, when he finished the letter, he typed—possibly upon another piece of paper—or possibly having then decided not to send the letter, he added it as a postscript. With morbid desire, doubtless to see how the words would look, and then destroy them, as of course he thought he did. The words, *'I hope I kill him—I want him to die—I'll be so glad—glad—'* Is that premeditated murder, or isn't it? He put what was in his mind there on the ribbon!"

The room was in confusion. Worthington sat clutching the arms of his chair. A stupid, fatuous grin was on his face, but his eyes were wide with terror. His composure wholly gone, he stammered:

"Why—why, that's a lie. I never wrote—"

The Doctor stood before him. "You see we've got you."

"No. Everything else you said was true. But this—this is a lie. I never saw the ribbon—"

A sardonic smile was on the Doctor's face. "Think well what you are saying, you know we'll use it against you. That ribbon contains your own individuality of typing."

For a moment Worthington was silent, struggling to master the emotion which had suddenly surged over him. "No," he said; and his voice now was calmer. "I never saw that ribbon. It wasn't on the machine when you found it."

"It was."

"Then you lie."

"Oh," said the Doctor, "do I? You forget—fortunately, Mr. Marberry was with me. So was Mr. Manton. Three of us together. That's good testimony that we found the ribbon. Your word, since you're being so highly technical, wouldn't go far against the oaths of the three of us."

Worthington eyed him. Again the man seemed coolly calculating, but his fingers gripping the chair arms were writhing.

The Doctor added, "You've had experience in pleading with the law. Think well. This is premeditated murder— you're going to the chair—I'll swear to that—"

"If I only had a lawyer," Worthington muttered as though to himself. "Say nothing—not now—only it's a damn lie—"

The Doctor caught the words. "There's a lawyer here. You see, I'm trying to settle it now."

A vague smile came to Worthington's bloodless lips. "I'm not a fool—your lawyer—"

"Not my lawyer—a member of the club who happens to

be here. You know the ethics of the legal profession—you know you may trust him—Mr. Rathburn."

Worthington got somewhat shakily to his feet. "You're right. You're no fool either. Damned clever, and damned—"

"Thank you," said the Doctor. "I want to be fair with you—fair but just."

Worthington flashed him a look; and sat apart with the Lawyer, whispering earnestly. Once he looked up and demanded:

"Are you going to present this evidence? Not give me a chance—"

"You deserve nothing," responded the Doctor sternly, "and you know it."

"You'll swear to it? To all this evidence?"

"I will."

The Lawyer said, "Will you, Sergeant Marberry?"

"Yes," said the detective.

"And you, Mr. Manton?"

"I will," Manton said. "He's lying to you—his last desperate stand. We found that ribbon—"

The Lawyer turned back. Again they conferred. Then Worthington spoke. "He tells me you have here the man who will be my prosecutor? You've thought of everything, haven't you? Do I understand that if I plead guilty—first degree murder—I won't get the chair?"

"You'll get it if you don't plead guilty," the Doctor assured him. They bargained. The young District Attorney could promise nothing except that he would do his best.

"Life," said Worthington. He said it with a sort of desperate weariness. "You've got me. Would I get off with life?"

"I think you would," the assistant district attorney agreed. "I'll do my best to save you."

"And—lifers have been pardoned? Good conduct—"

"Assuredly. It's your best course, Worthington."

He hesitated. Those near him heard him mutter, "That damned ribbon. But they've got me." He added aloud, with a snap of decision, "I'll plead guilty. Shall I sign it now?"

They wrote him a confession. He signed, and presently the detective had led him away. The Doctor gazed at the closing door with a faint smile.

"The typewriter told us many things, gentlemen, thanks to Mr. Manton. All of them were true—up to the finding of that ribbon. You see, we were morally certain of his intent to kill, but we could not prove it. So we forged that last vital link in the chain of evidence ourselves. He was the type of criminal who bargains with the law. We knew that from his record in England. We did not find that typewriter ribbon. He did not write those fatal words. But Marberry, Manton and I convinced him we would swear that he did, and he knew his best course was to yield."

The faint smile was still upon the detective's lips. "Would we have sworn falsely had he stood us off? I do not think so—I should not want that on my conscience. But he did not stand us off, because he was guilty. An innocent man would have held out to the end. And there, gentlemen, is something to think about. Guilt is always handicapped. You need only to know how to take advantage of its inherent weakness—and you have it beaten."

THE HOUSE OF DOOMED BRIDES

IN THE DIM past, a wizard-husband laid a potent spell upon the Frane women: Daughters they might have, but the mother's death must pay for every birth.... Yet Earle Kennison married Gretna Frane, and learned too late of the monstrous fate reserved for those who scoff!

The statement given here is filed among the official records of the London Branch, Scientific Club of Anglo-America. There are several brief affidavits attached to it: One from the attending physician; another, the opinion of a noted British Scientist; a seismograph record of the night in question from Clarkson Observatory, with a learned, technical and lengthy paper on the geological formation of the British Isles in relation to the possibility of earthquakes; an attempted psychical explanation of the strange affair, from a member of a Psychical Research Society; and a very earnest dissertation by a British clergyman who evidently felt called upon to review the case from a religious aspect.

All these papers are accessible to the public; anyone may find them as A-49371, "The Case of Sir Robert A—" I transcribe the main statement substantially in its official form. For obvious reasons attending publication, however, I have altered it both in names and dates—disguised it in other small details for the protection of a well-known English family.

— THE AUTHOR.

MY NAME IS Earle Kennison. Details of my early life, my family, are unimportant to this narrative; little is of interest before that August 4th, 19—which was my twentieth birthday. With Gretna Frane I was wholly in love, though I had not seen her or heard from her since the previous June. I did not, indeed, ever expect to see or to hear from her again. But on August 4th, unexpectedly, her note came. It gave me her home address—even that had heretofore been denied me. I stared at her few written words.

> I think, if you still love me, it will be all right for you to come. Oh, how I do hope so.
>
> Gretna.

I had known her at the University for two years. No family of hers had ever come to her school to take pride in her education. I knew little, almost nothing about her, for early in our friendship she bade me not inquire. Nor had she ever been willing to meet my family; nor would she have me speak of her to them.

A strange, queerly matured girl of sixteen, boarding at a school adjacent to mine. Small, slim, dark, with coal-black braids dangling like a child's. A singularly odd personality, half child, half woman, queerly intermingled. From the first, I had sensed an invisible black shroud of mystery

enveloping her. It seemed endowing her with a wistful-
ness—a settled, wan melancholy which all the laughter
of healthy girlhood could no more than drive into the
depths of her dark eyes. I had often noticed it lurking there.
Perhaps, to my own romantic youthfulness it was at first
an attraction. But soon I grew to fear it.

She did not seek my friendship. I realize now that
with all her little strength she was fighting always against
every normal instinct with which an abundant nature had
provided her—fighting, and losing.

That last night of June, I stood bidding her goodbye
for the summer vaca-
tion. Her hair was up
around her head in a
thick, black coil. I saw
her suddenly not as a

strange, wistful little child, but as a vibrant woman. And I felt myself a man. There was no need for love-making. It blazed from our eyes; it flowed like a stream between our fingers as they touched…. But she tore herself away; to separate us sprang the monster of that lurking tragedy in whose grip she was enveloped. Her plea was a sob of terror: "No! No, Earle—don't love me! No one must ever love me!"

I stared now, this August 4th, at her note. My promise, given at her tragic pleading that June night, was released. I could come to her—if I still loved her! I was on the Scotland train that night, bound for the small town near the border which she had named as her home.

THE VILLAGE OF Grath is an out-of-the-way place; it was mid-afternoon of August 5th before I reached its neighborhood. I dismissed my conveyance, walked the last half-mile through the somber forest alone, in a tumult of emotion….

And I stood at last before a small, crumbling stone gateway with an unhinged rusty gate, set off the main road at the end of a path which the summer vegetation had crept over and almost obliterated. A lost and forgotten spot in this new Twentieth Century. Here in the dark, hushed recesses of the enveloping forest I could have imagined the Black Prince standing with his huntsmen, imperiously winding his horn at these humble portals.

I pushed the tangle of ivy aside, entered, and saw the house. A castle such as might have graced a North Sea headland of Saxon England lay hidden here. But a castle all in miniature, for this was a small stone structure, looped and turreted but no larger than an unpretentious country home. Solemn and brooding, it stood enveloped in trees which, by contrast, seemed fantastic giants.

There was no garden about the little castle; no flowers, no paths save one leading from the gate to the small main doorway—a path with ferns and leaves and underbrush encroaching upon it unmolested.... The afternoon was overcast, windless, oppressive. I stood breathless in the heat, an intruder upon the past. It was as though all this had for centuries remained untouched by the hand of man. The gate through which I had passed, the little castle walls, stood with mute evidence of the fingers of Time plucking at them. Decrepit walls, crumbling stone, rusted ironwork, wormy wood, chipped and broken masonry.... Age everywhere; an aspect ancient, venerable, but all with a strange pathetic dignity, for in outward form, the building was unbroken save where perhaps the ivy mercifully hid its scars. A sturdy little castle in its bygone day, and still bravely standing.

How long I remained motionless with the ghosts of the past crowding me I do not know. But presently I was advancing, kicking away the forest creepers on the forgotten path. This was the home of Gretna Frane... her family.... What ancient tragic mystery was here? I could feel the specter of it standing at my elbow as I thumped the rusty knocker.

Then Gretna was in my arms; soft, clinging, with her lips on mine; her greeting ringing in my ears.

"Earle! You came! Earle, I think I dare say it now—I love you! I love you!"

No specter here! I held her, and the specter fled. I held

her with a surge of love; and in her kisses felt a love divine and a very human passion unrestrained.

"Earle! Let me go! I can't breathe!"

SHE LIVED ALONE with her grandfather. No servants— seldom, if ever, any visitors. I was to stay with them for a few days, they said. Amid the friendliness of their welcome, no questions were permitted me. A spirit of gayety was upon Gretna. I had never seen her like this. It brought to the interior of the castle a cheer and laughter which suddenly I knew was false. These ancient rooms, beamed oaken ceilings dull with the smoke of centuries; oak planks worn black and smooth beneath my feet—I was conscious always of their brooding age.

"After dinner this evening," the old man said, "we'll talk then, young Earle."

The night came; the long main hall, with its raised end whereon Gretna had set the black oak table for our evening meal, was shadowed in the candle-light. We sat over our coffee. Figures of a modern world—Gretna in a filmy dress of white; the old man erect and smiling in black dinner clothes for all the heat. Figures of a modern world; yet to me, the shadows of King Alfred and his fellows might have been dining there with us.

"You have been very patient, young Earle. You are all that Gretna said you were." His lean old hand went impulsively over mine on the table-top. "I like you. I only hope that perhaps this love you and Gretna have found may be allowed its fulfillment." His smile had faded; a shadow had swept to Gretna's face; I felt the specter nudging my side.

"Why, I thank you—" I began awkwardly, but he checked me.

"There was a reason why Gretna could not let herself love you—or anyone. I may, perhaps, have removed it now. I don't know. That, I think, we may find out—tonight." He added, "You've been patient; be patient a while longer. This family into which you would like to marry has a history—a tragic one. The present, young Earle, is but the past in the making. The future too, will advance to be the present, and fade away into the past. And we are—or at least we have been—a tragic family. It is that Gretna wanted to spare you—our fear of the future."

He would not let me speak. "No! It's your right to know the past—and if tonight we can just glimpse the future—"

I sat in the candle-light, and his slow, quiet old voice took me back among the shadows which all evening had been enveloping me....

"I was a handsome young devil when I was your age, young Earle, as handsome as you are, and as typical of that other half century as you are of this one. I came here to this house, wooing its young mistress. A motherless, fatherless girl—dark-eyed, black-haired, slight and beautiful—like Gretna. Her mother had died when she was born, her father had committed suicide with his grief. It seemed too bad, but not significant. I loved her, well, perhaps as you love Gretna.

"Our little girl, Gretna's mother, was born—and the birth killed my wife. I did not commit suicide—" His voice was quivering. "Perhaps I was too brave, or not brave enough. My wife died, and I put all my love into the little girl. She grew to maturity—at seventeen, like a small, dark rosebud. Like Gretna.... I told the young man when he came asking for her what I have told you. There were to be no children. Yet that was my own idea—against God's law—perhaps, too. That now is part of the punishment, for I made them promise.

"A coincidence? Or a physical defect of the women of our breed? There was no physician who honestly could say it was that…. My girl was married. She confessed afterward she yearned to have a child. She knew it would be a daughter." His voice raised sharply. "Gretna! You—as you know things are now—do you want to be a mother?"

I thrilled to Gretna's voice. "Yes! I do! Grandfather, you know I do!"

"That, poor young Earle, is perhaps the heritage of our women. Gretna says it frankly. You could not shake her in it…. Her mother died in giving her birth. Her father blamed himself. We found him dead, that earnest young man who had come asking me for her only a brief year before. Found him dead in the bottom of a ravine near here. I like to think he fell from the path above by accident. But I do not think so. And all these years I have watched Gretna maturing, her womanhood budding, swelling from springtime into summer, preparing to blossom—" His voice broke. "To blossom with our next tragedy."

SHE WAS HUDDLING now against him. His fingers stroked her hair, but his somber eyes held mine. "I had to tell her, warn her, years ago. I could not spare her. There is a tragedy in that, too. The mysteries life holds, the sorrow and conflict eternal—not to spare even childhood is in itself a tragedy. At fourteen, Gretna knew, that for her at least, love and marriage could only mean a child. A daughter, like an obsession, always that longing for a daughter. That was more than pathetic, tragic. Why, at fourteen I found—when I had always been so careful to keep dolls away from her—at fourteen, I found her once crooning to a little thing of rags she had made...."

I sat staring, unblinking, with eyes that smarted in the smoke of my neglected cigarette. This blight upon a breed of women, each to bear another like herself, and die! What destiny was this? What power greater than all our little mortal strivings, was exacting this penalty? And why?... And now I had come like a wind-blown puppet to play my part!

Mysterious workings of nature! Awesome, unfathomable business! A physical defect of these women, an understandable, medical fact unquestionably. Yet back of it, must there not be the guiding hand of Omnipotence? The innocent shall suffer for the guilty. Back, somewhere in this line, had been woman's sin, no doubt. And the innocent shall suffer—

Woman's sin? It was almost as though I had spoken the thought aloud, so that the old man was moved to answer it. His quiet gaze was on my face. He said:

"I have not told you quite all, young Earle. There was a tale my wife told me. She was motherless, fatherless. A tale told to her by the old family nurse. Perhaps it was only from a generation previous—or perhaps from several generations, so that it had come down like a legend.

"An old woman's fancy? Call it that, young Earle. I would not have you believe it. My wife believed it. And to me it has become very real."

Gretna had come close beside me. I felt her trembling. It was real to her also, this thing the old man was about to disclose. His eyes held me.

"There was a time when one of the women of this family cast off her husband. Her child was to be born, but its father was a man of evil, a necromancer, by profession a juggler of the secrets of nature. A juggler of things evil, who put his skill to such evil purpose indeed, that he ended by being hanged upon the gallows. His wife had previously left him, when first she learned what manner of man he really was.

"And for that, he cursed her. A tangible human curse, young Earle, a curse laid upon her and her issue with all the man's human hatred and his power of necromancy. A curse, so that she in childbirth, must die—and her daughter live on, in turn to die… Gretna child, stop shuddering…."

I held Gretna closer. The old man said, "That is nothing but the tale of a servant woman, told to my wife. You need not believe it. But imagination is a very strange thing. To me—"

He was obviously trying to speak lightly now. His lips showed the trace of a grim smile. "To me—so many years have I brooded on it—that man of evil who laid so diabolical a curse upon a line of women—he is very real to me now. In fancy I conjure him, a fellow in doublet and hose, with lean face and burning eyes. So real that sometimes, Gretna and I fancy that the evil specter of him still hovers within these walls."

The specter of him here within these walls? How could I doubt it? I, who ever since I had been here had felt a specter nudging at my side! Imagination! Call it that, you who read this, and toss away the menace. But I, who was there, could not, with every word of the old man, that apparition hovering near me became more real. A man… I stared across the shadowy room. The thing was here with us now! Doublet and hose. Long and lean and evil face. Eyes that burned and leered at me with a gloating, fury. Eyes seeing its new victim....

But I tried to fling away the vision. I heard my voice crying aloud in the welter of my thoughts. "If the decision is mine, I want Gretna! She—I'll protect her—she shall remain the last of her line. We'll stamp it out, whatever it is—Gretna and I the last of our line—"

"No!" burst from Gretna. "I want—I must have my little daughter—"

I was on my feet. What I would have said I do not know. Old Frane raised his hand sharply. "Wait, young Earle! You and Gretna, so young, thinking you must decide the future! That's decided for us, lad! Sit down, Earle—"

He pushed Gretna gently away; he smiled at her and at me. "We sent for you, young Earle, because I think that tonight I shall be able to let us glimpse what the future holds. Perhaps if we knew what lay ahead of us three we could advance to meet it more courageously—"

He was speaking quite calmly now. "This is not wholly mysticism, lad. I am no seer, but—what you did not know—I have been in my day, well, to some extent, a scientist. Yet even in science, a measure of mysticism creeps. For years, as I watched Gretna's womanhood unfolding, I have wanted to know the future. To transport myself ahead of my time—with a drug, a mechanism, a crystal ball—anything with which even for an instant, I could lift the veil.

"The past is less difficult to envisage. It hovers always quite close to us. The future is equally as real an entity.

Advancing into reality, as the past recedes…. Why, Gretna! You were happy over this when we sent for Earle!"

But she was shuddering now. White and silent and shuddering. Was it a premonition, a sense beyond the normal, which already was giving her a glimpse of what our future held? I think it was that. And upon me too, the future was resting an impalpable, icy hand… or was it the specter of that nameless thing which I sensed always was in the room with us. Was that what was touching me now? I started into sudden physical alertness as though I had felt a ponderable touch. Or was it a wraith conjured only by my thoughts, perhaps? A gloating, menacing thing, with burning eyes watchful of our movement…?

"Come," said old Frane. "Come, Gretna—let us see—"

AT THE INQUEST they pounded me with scientific questions which I could not answer because I am no scientist. And if I were, the confusion of those moments, my own stress of emotion, would befog me out of all credibility as a witness. Did old Frane explain to me any scientific principle for the conquering of Time? Did he talk of Time and Space as one blended Entity? Yes, that I remember. Time was to be crossed like Space. As though there could be a geography of Time; as though the Future were a Location in Time, to which we could move at least our Minds….

I know definitely, and I testified, that he led us to Gretna's bedroom. A place sanctified by her girlhood. Her little bed, a dressing table, a chair…. A faint perfume in the air which to me had come to mean her. A dim, sanctified place, shadowed now with shadows that moved as he set down the candelabra he had carried in to light our entrance.

"This, young Earle, is the room in which Gretna was born. To me, it is redolent of the past—"

The crowding past! I could feel it pressing around us. This emptiness here—an emptiness crowded with the past. And the future! I became aware that the future was here, as well as the past. Crowded empty Space, with only Time to hold separate its myriad events....

Three of us here, the old man, Gretna, and I. No! We were four! Those watchful eyes still were upon us. I could feel, rather than see, them. Yet how easy, here in these flickering shadows of the candlelight, to conjure that lean and evil face—that evil man of doublet and hose! Hovering shape from the Past, stalking us here in the Present—ready to go with us now into the Future....

The mechanism stood on a small table. A crystal ball? It seemed no more than that. It stood a foot high in the center of the table, poised on a small wooden base. I recall that to my mind, for all those uneasy specters of which I was so utterly conscious, there sprang a vague contempt. This old fellow—half mad, or wholly mad perhaps—was no more than a charlatan, a necromancer. And a sudden hope came to me. Was all this tragedy a figment of his own warped brain? Was Gretna his dupe? And now, for his own unreasoning, irrational purpose, was he trying to make me a victim too?

But the thing was more than a crystal ball. At each corner of the table stood a small apparatus, a tiny brazier, like an ash-tray. A light-shield stood in front of it, and above, a small lens, held horizontal in a bracket. Over that, a mirror; and a tiny prism, and a small metal cylinder like the barrel of a microscope, pointed at the crystal ball. At each corner of the table, the small cylinders pointed at the crystal ball.

We sat by the table. Frane said, "This apparatus would not operate without your being here, young Earle, because quite evidently your future is interwoven with ours. Without your consciousness to advance with ours beyond the veil, it resisted us. So we sent for you. Gretna, sit by him, child—"

We sat together. Her trembling body huddled against me. Her fingers as she clung to mine were dank with the premonitory chill of death.…The old man stood behind us. He moved about the table; into each of the little braziers, from a glass vial, he poured a small quantity of powder.… The touch of Gretna's fingers seemed to communicate their chill to me.…Was this science, or something diabolical or both? To lift the veil which the Almighty in His infinite wisdom has placed between us and our future—was this thing permissible? Or was it something that man may not do?

With a puff, old Frane blew out the candle. The darkness sprang like a monster with a great black cloak flung over us.… The old man was fumbling with matches. Gretna sobbed, "Earle, I'm afraid!"

A match lighted with its yellow flare; showed me the old man's grim face; bloodless lips; gleaming, eager eyes, probing a mystery no man may probe! Eyes that sought to see the unseeable! His old fingers were trembling with eagerness as he held the match to one of the braziers. The powder ignited. It burned with a dull purple light—a slow, steady glow. In a moment, all four of the braziers were lighted. The lens caught the glow, projected it upward in a tiny, concentrated beam; bent by the mirror to the horizontal; through the prism, into the projecting cylinder—a beam spread flat like a tiny rainbow of weirdly confused color, yet all dimly purple.

The old man's voice was saying, "In that burning powder is the secret of Time. A purple beam of vibrations to overtake the seconds, the minutes, days and years—"

I SCARCELY HEARD him. Gretna was stiff beside me. The crystal was dim in the flat shadow from the brazier shields. Then from each of the pointing cylinders at the table corners, the purple beam sprang forth. I was aware that the old man had opened tiny shutters to release it. The crystal was bathed in their strangely lurid glow. One of them, from behind me, passed close by my shoulder. I sensed a vibration from it. A soundless whirr; a breath of impalpable heat....

I bent to Gretna. "Don't be afraid. It's nothing—"

A burning powder. I could smell it now like some heavy, exotic incense. It seemed to make my head reel as I breathed it. Was this a trick? A madman's trick to drug my senses—make me think I saw what I did not?

"Ah—" His sigh was exultant. The clear depths of the crystal were filled with purple shadows. Taking form; tiny images—myself, in them—my intent face, with Gretna beside me. Vague outlines of the room in miniature.

"Ah! You see? See us three? That is the present, but in a moment it will move forward. Slowly, at first—then faster, rushing us into the future!"

Wholly mad or at best a trickster! Of course the present was mirrored in the crystal. A reflection of us as we sat at the table was all I was seeing.

There was just an instant when an utter terror swept me. I felt that I was about to see what I had no right to see. And I was afraid. But whatever the crystal was about to disclose, its secret remained forever hidden. Yet what a vaster thing unfolded! Frane was no trickster, for he was now as frightened, as surprised as Gretna and myself. The four purple-glowing braziers reflected a dim glow everywhere about the room. The perfume of the burning powder was escaping, and so was the light. Not confined to the tiny beams, but glowing everywhere; and everywhere seeming to gain intensity. Something was going wrong! And suddenly to my consciousness, the crystal ball, the four mechanisms, the table—everything, all of us—were lost in a wild glare of purple light. Like a living monster, it had escaped its confining prisms and projectors. The air around me was tingling, snapping. A hum filled my ears; then a roaring. A numbness had come to me. A lightness of body; physical chains dropping away. A wild sense of freedom; my senses were fading. I heard the sound of old Frane as his body fell to the floor with a choking cry; felt Gretna sag against me, and vaguely felt myself slump inert in my chair. This thing—this science—was a Frankenstein monster risen to destroy us!

But my consciousness went on. Will you who read this think me mad? Or lying? It does not matter—I can only tell what I remember....

A dim, glowing chaos was around me. Melting shadows; formless movement; a soundless humming; and within me a faint tingling to mark a spark of the physical still remaining.

Formless shadows for what seemed an endless time. But

they were shadows of old Frane, and Gretna, and me. The sound of music; slim little Gretna standing beside me, white-robed. Our marriage—it swept by as though upon the whirring wings of fancy. Yet it was very real. An instant impression, dissolving, crowding into other shadows of its kind.

A bedroom—this bedroom, in which, like a dead shell I could feel my body slumped in purple light.... This bedroom—Gretna, my wife... Ah! That fleeting vision of love melting into other visions, nearly always here in this room. This crowded space, yielding now its future secrets! Within these walls....

Then I knew these were not visions. I was living these fragments.... Whirling forward through them, leaving them behind me as memories.... Riding upon a winged steed....

A CORNER OF the beamed ceiling showed a wide, opening crack. Water had come through in the heavy rain. Gretna said, "Earle darling, we really ought to repair this old house. Grandfather never would. He never will, if you leave it to him."

And I said, "Yes." And kissed her....

Another year....

"I noticed that last year, Earle. It's getting really too old, this house—"

Last year. This year. And other years. They sped away. Happy years, with only a shadow of fear upon them. But it was a shadow made more vivid by the sunlight of our happiness. Gretna, my wife, old Frane, myself, living here. The house and all of us were getting older. No children had come to bless us... Ah! One now was coming. I was very happy, but the shadow stalked me closer....

Shadow? It had always been with me, a vague nameless weight upon my heart, a shadow of fear upon my happiness. But when I was told that a child was coming, the shadow suddenly leaped again into form—the face, horribly familiar now, leering at me. Jibing! Did I hear the voice? It seemed that there was a voice, a taunt, a gloating mocking taunt, hideously terrible....

The months went by... The nurse said: "A perfect, wonderful little girl, like her mother." But I burst into the room, shuddering. She was still alive, my Gretna, there in the bed, her face with closed eyes a white waxen mask.... The baby was crying with its puny new-born wail. The doctor said gravely, "We had—she had rather a bad time, but it's all right now. Rather a bad time, eh, nurse?"

But it wasn't all right. The doctor said, "You go now. I'll call you if we need you." It wasn't all right, and I stumbled out to sit with old Frane.... And presently the nurse called, hastily, with alarm in her tone.... And I went back—

"Earle, my husband—" Her dear voice, dim with distance as it rode away on her bravely riding spirit. "Earle, take care of our little daughter—don't be too sorry, about me...."

Desolation. Loneliness.... And then, in the black darkness of my stricken life, the jibing monster out of the past revealed itself with a sudden, complete clearness. Monstrous, triumphant apparition, dangling here over me with outstretched arms; fingers quivering as though raining upon me the full measure of its curse. And my head rang now unmistakably with its eerie jibing voice. Horrible mocking laughter. Diabolic triumph—noisome with evil—noisome with the stench of the grave....

I sat numbed, beaten and pounded at last to where no

longer had I the strength of mind even to be terrified....
Emptiness, filled only with jostling memories. Here in this
bedroom the still, white shape of Gretna lying now in bed.
Old Frane had fallen with his grief.... The infant lay in its
bassinet with a white aura around it....

I was trembling. Or was it the floor beneath me which
was trembling? The room was filled with a purple glow. A
light run rampant. It seemed to be eating at the floor, the
walls, the ceiling, eating like soundless purple flame. The
room, the house was shuddering. Old Frane staggered to
his feet.

I gasped: "An earthquake! It's shaking us—"

I heard his wild laugh. A rumble sounded outside. Something fell. Crashed. The house was crumbling—falling. Ten
years! It had not seemed ten years since Gretna and I were
married. But it was. And the old house had come to its end.
A rift somewhere, a last crumbling keystone, a foundation
twisting, sliding. The old house was falling....

Something heavy hit my shoulder. I was on my feet. I
must get Gretna out. I ran to the bed. Lifted her up, held
her so white and soft against me. A cloud of falling debris
enveloped old Frane; but I was past it, staggering with
Gretna so white and soft in my arms. The infant was buried
in a choking cloud. The purple glow was gone; the house
rocked, clattered behind me as I escaped out into the starlight. Into the cool air of dawn, where to the east, over the
forest, a pink flush was mounting.

My head cleared. Normality came to me. Under the trees
beside the line of willows, the castle lay a tumbled mass
of ruins. I sank down insensible beside Gretna, and there
they found as....

THEY TELL ME they found the castle in ruins; found Frane's body, but no infant. And there was no earthquake. It was only August 6th. I had been in the castle, so they say, only over night.

My physician examined me. I was twenty years old when I entered that castle. But I was thirty, that next morning when I emerged. I looked thirty. The police said it was only mental shock. But I know I lived those ten years, crowded into that one night of the world's slow-moving Time. And my physician says I aged ten years. Not only my looks. My organs had aged. My arteries, my blood-pressure had changed as only the living of ten years could change them.

Gretna, too, physicians say, was a woman of twenty-six that next morning. Evidently that much, at least, is an established fact. Gretna's memory of those ten years we lived together in the old castle agrees with mine.

There is little more to tell. Gretna and I were married in London a few days later. Our child, our little daughter, was born the following year. Who could ask me to picture what agony of mind was mine those hours while I waited for what the doctors would tell me? The child lived. Ah! I had known it would! But Gretna? For days she hovered upon the brink. Then she was restored to me. Several years have passed now. Gretna lives, healthy, happy with me in the treasure of our daughter.

For this that I have recounted we ask no one's credulity. Have we an explanation? Yes; it is this:

Before each of us, in life, the future stretches like an open road. At every instant of our life there are branch roads turning from it. A word, a deed, and we plunge down one of them. The course we take—that is the route of our life to the destiny we each of us makes for himself.

And we think, Gretna and I, that upon the old castle and its inmates lay that curse. A spell of evil, call it what you will; something not to be denied. But within those walls the family of Gretna Frane was doomed to disaster.

We lived there, man and wife, for ten years. And the ravages of time, those ten years, were too much for the crumbling old structure. It fell, and with it fell the curse. As though the jibing monster himself were engulfed, his evil spirit falling with those walls. And Gretna and I were released. By a merciful Providence, we have been given those ten years to live again.

You who read this may well say, "Ah, now you are actually living those ten years. You lived them that night in the castle only in fancy—a fancy born of your own imagination, or perhaps under the spell of a drug from old Frane's strange device."

Perhaps so. Perhaps we lived them in fancy! Lived them, to put them in the past, with vivid memories remaining! Perhaps that is all life is! Metaphysicians have said so. I do not know.

But I think, of all the learned reviews of our strange experience, the Reverend Abercrombie comes nearest to the truth. Gretna thinks so too; and to woman is given a spiritual insight which few men possess. The Reverend Abercrombie says, "Science is sometimes too presumptuous. There are some things about which we seek to know too much."

I am coming now to believe that is so.

EARLE KENNISON.

IN THE MURDERER'S BRAIN

IN THE MID-FORTIES of New York City, not far from Fifth Avenue, stands the huge building which houses the Scientific Crime Club.

The club's luxurious quarters are on the roof, far removed from the turmoil of busy city streets. There is a little garden of pebbled winding paths between flower beds and trellises, with a splashing fountain in its center.

One of the rooms has sliding walls and roof which in pleasant weather may be opened to the sky. And there are other rooms of luxurious leather lounging chairs, a little bar and restaurant with white-coated attendants.

Bridge and chess tables are here; a billiard room; a small bowling alley; a shooting gallery; a small gymnasium and pool.

Outwardly they are rooms for wealthy men at play.

But some of them are very strangely equipped.

One is crowded with expensive devices of modern science; an electrical laboratory; a room equipped for research chemistry and physics. And there is a room which would seem to be a theatrical storehouse—scenery, props of every imaginable kind, ranged in an orderly litter. They are the club's equipment when it is at work.

No one, visiting the club for the first time, would think of it as more than a playground.

But the lighting effects of its rooms can be made extraordinary, for they have wiring as intricate as any theatrical stage.

There are ingenious secret panels in some of the walls; hidden traps in the floor and the roof—an amazing equipment which may not be used for a year but is always available for the scientific probing of the minds of suspected criminals who may be brought here.

The club members, largely, are wealthy professional men. Upon a warm summer night, a group of them were gathered in one of the lounging rooms.

Some club members were here by chance; others had been summoned as spectators and participants, in a case which just today had come before the club.

The services of the members—the resources of the

"It's a lie! I didn't do it!"

club—have for years been at the disposal of the police, or any individual who cares to demand them.

The cases come at irregular intervals, generally from the police of New York City and its outlying districts—clueless affairs, usually, with definite suspects upon whom, by ordinary police methods, guilt would probably never be fastened.

The case, tonight, was typical. The Psychologist, lounging in his chair with his fellow members around him, was saying:

"It's a pathetic affair, gentlemen. The girl—she was only sixteen—killed herself last evening. And perhaps almost simultaneously, her father was murdered."

"How do you know she killed herself?" the Banker demanded. "Why not a double murder?"

"The facts are against it," the Psychologist said. "The thing happened in Maple Grove—just about this time last evening. Peter Mackenzie and his daughter, Alice. They lived in a small but very respectable lodging house. He was a widower—a glass blower in the Torrence Glass Works out there. And the girl kept house for him."

"SHE TOOK POISON, I understand," the Doctor interjected.

"Why?" asked the Very Young Man eagerly. "Was she a pretty girl, Dr. Allaire?"

"They say she was," the Psychologist answered. "An old-fashioned sort of girl. Her father brought her here from Scotland, just after she was born. The father was a man of fifty. You know the type—industrious, thrifty, squarely solid both in physical build and in character. A plain man, of doggedly high principles. And he brought his daughter up in just that fashion. They say the girl was dutiful, gentle, sweet—"

"And she killed herself," the Very Young Man sighed. "I wish I had known her. Maybe then—"

"At nine o'clock last evening," the Psychologist went on, "Peter Mackenzie is known to have gone out and left his daughter at home. They were both agitated—the landlady heard their voices, but nothing that they said. At ten o'clock she went up to see Alice. The girl was lying on her bed, unconscious from an overdose of sedative. She never recovered consciousness; she died at dawn today. And last night—at nine-thirty while the girl was ending her life—less than two miles away her father was being murdered."

"And there is a clear connection?" the Lawyer asked.

"There is indeed." The gray-haired, distinguished-looking Psychologist sat up in his chair, smoothing a crumpled bit of paper in his hand. "Here is the note she left—pathetic, simple words. He read:

Father darling— He doesn't love me, so why bother? I hope you tell him so. But even as much as I love you, I cannot live without him. Oh please forgive me—

THERE WAS A brief silence, the men staring as the Psychologist put the smudged, tear-stained bit of paper back into his pocket. Then the Lawyer said:

"It seems obvious that her father went to meet the man she loved."

"Exactly," the Psychologist agreed. "That inference is plain. They met. And the unknown man killed Mackenzie—on a bridge high over the Central Railroad tracks in the outskirts of Maple Grove. We have a witness to it. The 9:28 train for New York had just left the Maple Grove station.

"It wasn't going very fast when it reached the bridge. The engineer plainly saw two men high up there—the silhouettes of them. He saw the murderer shoving Mackenzie—and saw Mackenzie come hurtling down—striking, not the track on which the train was advancing, but the one adjacent. The fall killed him. The murderer perhaps had intended to throw him in front of the train—"

"If the engineer saw the murderer, what did he look like?" the Lawyer demanded.

"Just a bareheaded silhouette. No details. The silhouette of a man peering down; then running away. Now gentlemen, you can see easily why Marberry, of Maple Grove, referred the case to us. This man whom the little Alice loved more than her father or her life—only she and her father knew his identity. And there you have the murder motive. This stern old Scotchman, meeting this man—"

"The murderer felt that he could control the girl?" the Astronomer suggested.

"Or perhaps he would have murdered her later," the Psychologist said. "Her suicide saved him the trouble. The case, gentlemen, by inference, is extraordinarily simple. But that, indeed, is exactly why the police are balked. There are no tangible clues. Nothing but inference—an assumption of what happened and why it happened."

"Which wouldn't get very far before a jury," the Lawyer interjected. "Defense counsel would knock that sort of evidence into a cocked hat."

"Exactly," the Psychologist agreed. "We have the suspects—and nothing else. It wasn't hard, even in a few short hours today, for Marberry to locate the possible men for whom Alice Mackenzie could have had this attachment.

"There are only two. A young fellow named George Bolton who works in an office here in New York; and a rich widower of thirty—an ex-actor named Thomas Dale, who was fortunate in a mining speculation and now has retired from business. Both were seen frequently in the girl's company—old Mackenzie seemed to like them both."

"And where were they last evening?" the Lawyer demanded.

The Psychologist smiled wryly.

"Marberry has been grilling them all day. Young Bolton was in his Maple Grove boarding house room—on the ground floor so that he could easily have gone in and out the window without attracting attention. Thomas Dale was alone in his Maple Grove apartment, with a private entrance to the street so that no one but himself can say whether he was there all evening or not."

"And it's up to us to make the choice," the Very Young Man exclaimed. "But how in the devil—"

"I've sent for them," the Psychologist said. "They'll be here any minute. Now gentlemen, there is little for you to do—most of it negative. You may hear, for instance, a queer grinding, clicking noise. Ignore it! Pretend it does not exist. I want the murderer perhaps to think he is imagining it."

The Psychologist's lean, sensitive face was grim now as he added:

"The guilt is in the brain of one of these two men. I'm going to drag it out—without him knowing it."

A club attendant appeared at the door of the room. "George Bolton is here to see Dr. Allaire."

"Send him in." The Psychologist stood up. "The idea is, gentlemen," he added hurriedly, "I've told both these suspects that a wealthy, eccentric criminologist is interested in the case—that he is convinced they are both innocent—has hired me scientifically to demonstrate it. Whether they believe that or not is immaterial. Neither dared refuse to come. So you gentlemen act with the assumption of sympathy. An experiment in applied psychology—to prove innocence, not guilt. And we will—"

GEORGE BOLTON ENTERED the room and stood staring, surprised, confused by the number of men all of whom were gazing at him intently. He was a tall, blond, broad-shouldered, very handsome young fellow, dressed in a neat dark business suit.

"Dr.—Allaire?" he said hesitantly.

"I am Dr. Allaire," the Psychologist said. He indicated a chair. "Sit down, please. Thank you for coming, Mr. Bolton."

The young man smiled. "Oh—how do you do? I thought I'd gotten into the wrong room."

"These gentlemen are my fellow club members," the Psychologist explained. "I need not introduce them by name. Gentlemen, this is Mr. Bolton. The police seem to think he might be guilty of the crime I've been describing to you."

Young Bolton smiled nervously at the men as he sat down. "The police have been pretty tough on me all day. What is it you want of me, Dr. Allaire? Lord knows I've already told—"

Again the attendant appeared. "Mr. Thomas Dale is here, Dr. Allaire."

"Send him in, Arthur."

At the name, young Bolton had leaped to his feet. "Dale? Why, you didn't tell me—what is this, some more inquisition?"

"No," the Psychologist smiled. "Quite the reverse. Sit down, Mr. Bolton. The police told me that was one of your troubles—you're too impetuous. If I can prove your innocence, you'll be free of the police. Don't you understand? As things are, they can't prove a thing but they'll hound you, trying and hoping—"

But the young man wasn't listening. With flushed face, he stared at the door where now Thomas Dale stood calmly surveying the room.

"Dr. Allaire?"

"I am Dr. Allaire. Come in, Mr. Dale."

The Psychologist introduced the club members. The

second suspect was an extreme contrast to young Bolton—a man of thirty, short but powerfully built. His dark hair was thinning at the temples. His smooth-shaven face of rugged features, was somewhat pale. He had been an actor, and it showed now in the self-possession with which he acknowledged the introductions. And then his quiet gaze landed upon Bolton who was standing with clenched fists.

"How do you do, Bolton?" he said. "I didn't know you had been invited here. Where do you want me to sit, Dr. Allaire?"

Certainly there was no love lost between the two men. The Psychologist placed them in small chairs, side by side. They were diagonally facing the intent group of club members, with the Psychologist standing before them.

"I owe you both an explanation," he began quietly. "I have been commissioned to try and produce some evidence that will persuade the police to let you alone. My client is aware that there is no evidence against either of you—"

"Who is your client?" Bolton asked. "Is he here? No one is interested in me—"

"I am not at liberty to name him," the Psychologist said. "Perhaps it is myself? Why not? I am interested—well, to be frank, if not in you two, certainly in applied psychology."

He smiled at the two men, who now were staring at him with an almost breathless intentness. And it was obvious that both of them considered his words as a preface to some new questioning with the same purpose the police had had all day.

One was guilty? One innocent? No choice could be made from their outward aspect. Wholly different types, they had balked the police: young Bolton with an impetuous angry flush, or grim sullenness; and Thomas Dale with a seemingly quiet desire to give all the information he could, and an imperturbable self-possession.

"It is not my purpose to question you," the Psychologist went on. "A man—as the police have told you—was seen killing Peter Mackenzie. Unfortunately the witness cannot describe that man. It could have been either of you—or anyone of a thousand other men—"

"Which is very hard on us," Dale said.

"It is indeed. I quite agree with you. To come to the point—I have invited these gentlemen here as witnesses to an experiment in psychology— Wait a minute, Mr. Bolton—don't interrupt me, please. You are both inno-cent—you have told the police so. And both of you know by now, very well indeed, that there is not a particle of evidence against either one of you—"

He paused, and then he abruptly added:

"You don't know, do you, anything of what happened between Mackenzie and his murderer on that bridge?"

"I do not," Bolton said.

"How could I?" Dale said.

"My idea is, to tell you what happened," the Psycholo-gist continued. He smiled faintly. "Not that I know what happened, because I don't. But what I tell you, I want you to remember. Will you try?"

"I don't understand—" Dale began. Then, both he and Bolton nodded dubiously. The watching men could not miss the fact that both were frightened. But still there could be no choice: a guilty man, afraid of exposure—but an innocent man would also be afraid that by some mischance he would be incriminated.

"Yes," they both said. And Dale added, "I'll try my best to do whatever you suggest."

"Thanks."

An abrupt tenseness seemed to come to the room as the Psychologist took a folded sheet of paper from his pocket, and adjusted his glasses.

"I have here some notes I made on what probably happened up there on the bridge. I am going to read them to you—I want you to listen carefully. The theory is—into your empty mind I am going to put these facts. They are quite simple. I want you to engrave them there in your brain."

HE STARED AT the flushed young Bolton and the pale Thomas Dale. Perhaps one of them now had a wild desire to withdraw, but if so, he did not dare show it.

"Are you ready?" the Psychologist added quietly.

Again they both nodded. Very slowly, with careful but drab intonation which emphasized no word, the Psychologist read:

"The murderer led his victim onto the bridge. They talked in the moonlight about Alice. They were angry. The murderer said, 'I never made love to her.' Then they sat on the bench by the rail and the victim said, 'But it is not like my child. You cannot make me believe it.' The victim was toying with a blue cap in his hand. Then a moment later the murderer pushed him over the rail. He fell to the railroad track and lay crumpled between the gleaming rails with the moonlight bathing him."

The room was heavily silent as the Psychologist paused. And looking up from his notes, he added: "That's clear, isn't it? I want you to memorize it, not necessarily word for word, but the exact sense of it. I'll read it again."

Even more slowly, more drably than before, he repeated it. And then at once added:

"You, Jack Bruce—"

From across the room the Very Young Man looked startled.

"Yes, sir?"

"Just beyond that door—" the Psychologist gestured, "I put a small table with some articles on it. Bring it in, will you please? Carefully, Jack—"

The Very Young Man hastened to obey, and came back at once from the adjoining room dragging a small square table with a group of miscellaneous articles spread upon it.

"Here you are, Dr. Allaire."

"Thanks, Jack."

The Psychologist drew the table before young Bolton and Thomas Dale who stared at it silently. Without speaking, the Psychologist touched a switch. The roomlights faded. Shadows enveloped all the intent men, and from the ceiling a narrow white beam of light came down to illumine the table with the objects lying there fully revealed in the white glare.

The Psychologist was in the shadow. Close at the edge of the circle of white illumination young Bolton and Dale sat staring, fascinated. There were perhaps twenty objects arranged on the table. They were all commonplace, seemingly without any relation to each other: Dr. Allaire's personal card; an envelope and letterhead of the Scientific Crime Club; a man's brown felt hat and gloves; a silver-headed cane; an old battered doll; a blue knitted little cape; a few coins—

From the shadows, the Psychologist said quietly: "My idea is to put into your mind a knowledge of these things, almost all of which are wholly unrelated to the crime."

"That was Alice's doll," young Bolton said abruptly.

"Yes," Dale agreed. "I've seen it. She said she had it most of her life—she treasured it."

"I have no purpose of trying to find out which of them you recognize," the Psychologist said: "That is—quite—"

He let his voice trail away; and in the silence of the shadowed room now, a very faint sound was audible. A low grinding, clinking sound. It was muffled—indescribably queer. It lasted no more than five seconds.

In the darkness someone shifted his feet as though startled. Dale and Bolton both murmured something, but the Psychologist's voice had only stopped for those five seconds, and now he was talking again:

"The things on that table have no relation to each other—" He moved forward into the white glare and shoved the table away. "Forget them. I want you only to remember what happened on the bridge between the victim and the murderer. I read it to you twice—"

FROM HIS POCKET he took two pencils and two small pads of writing paper, and handed them to young Bolton and Dale.

"You can scribble in the darkness," he said. "And neither can see what the other is writing. Put your name at the top—and then write your memory of what I read you."

"Well—" Dale murmured.

"I may get it wrong," Bolton said.

"Do your best."

Neither of them wrote hastily. It was several minutes before they had finished.

"Here you are," Bolton said. Dale handed his silently.

The Psychologist took the two scrawled papers. In the silence of the shadowed room several of the men tensely shifted themselves in their chairs. Thomas Dale and young Bolton were dim blobs in the gloom. At the circle of white glare, beating down on the floor now where the table had been, the Psychologist stood in shadow.

FOR A MOMENT he silently read what the two men had written.

"This is very interesting, gentlemen." There was just a hint of emotion vibrating in his voice. "A comparison of these two little essays with my original will interest you all very much indeed. To refresh your memories. I'll read you again my exact, original words which Mr. Bolton and Mr. Dale attempted to reproduce."

"I can't be sure—" Dale murmured out of the darkness.

"Don't interrupt me now, please," the Psychologist retorted sharply. He was holding his original paper into the light. "Here was what I asked them to reproduce:

"The murderer led his victim onto the bridge. They talked in the moonlight about Alice. They were angry. The murderer said, 'I never made love to her.' They then sat on the bench by the rail and the victim said, 'But it is not like my child. You cannot make me believe it.' The victim was toying with a blue cap in his hand. Then a moment later the murderer pushed him over the rail. He fell to the railroad track and lay crumpled between the gleaming rails with the moonlight bathing him."

"There is the original. Now here is what one of them wrote. Analyze it carefully, gentlemen.

" 'The murderer took his victim to the bridge. They stood in the starlight and they talked angrily about Alice. The murderer said, 'I did not ever make love to her.' They were sitting by the rail and Mackenzie said. 'My child is not like that. I don't believe it.' He was toying with something blue in his hand. Then suddenly the murderer shoved him over the rail. He fell and lay crumpled on the gleaming railroad track bathed by the starlight.' "

From the darkness of the intent room, as the Psychologist paused, came the Lawyer's voice.

"He seems to have made several errors, Dr. Allaire, but I don't exactly see what—"

"Let me analyze them for you. Please be quiet, you two— no apologies are necessary for your errors. This writer says starlight instead of moonlight. He says they were sitting by the rail. I mentioned that they sat on the bench by the rail. He says Mackenzie was toying with something blue in his hand. I said it was a blue cap, but he evidently forgot that."

The Psychologist was talking swiftly now. "So much for that one, gentlemen. Now I'll read you the other.

" 'The murderer and his victim went out onto the bridge. It was moonlight and they talked about the girl and the murderer said, 'But I did not ever make love to her.' They were sitting on the box by the rail. Mackenzie was toying with a blue cape in his hand and the murderer said, 'It is not my child—you cannot make me believe it.' Then the murderer pushed him through the rail and he fell to the track with the gleaming headlight bathing him.' "

A startled gasp had come from several of the men in the

darkness. "Gentlemen," the Psychologist added, "which is the guilty version?"

"That one!" Several of them chorused it.

"No question of it," the Psychologist said crisply. "Lights, Marberry please."

A glare of lights sprang in the room. Thomas Dale was sitting pale, intent, awestruck. Young George Bolton was on his feet, flushed, trembling, with a hand flung before his eyes in the glare.

"It's a lie!" he cried. "I didn't do it! I didn't mean to write those things. I don't know what possessed me—"

"The guilt in your brain possessed you," the Psychologist said ironically. "There's your man, Marberry."

From the doorway the bulky uniformed police sergeant sprang forward, gripping the terrified Bolton.

"So they got you—an' I couldn't! Come on—out with it—you can't lie out of this."

"I can—I mean there isn't anything to lie out of. You take your hands off me!"

"I found out more about him this afternoon," the sergeant said. "He's been making love to an heiress over in Pleasant Hills. I located her—dragged it out of her."

"That's a lie!" Bolton stood struggling in the sergeant's grip.

"Oh, is it?" Marberry said. "Well you'll get a chance to tell her that before the D.A."

Then Bolton suddenly broke. "All right, I did it. You let me alone, I tell you. Stop torturing me—all of you—let me alone. Gloria's right—I am engaged to her—her father knows it—"

"And poor little Alice Mackenzie with her coming child,

and her dogged, outraged father—they were the obstacles," the Psychologist said. "A murder motive as old as history. And despicable beyond most murder motives. Take him away, Marberry."

AND WHEN THE room had quieted, the Psychologist said:

"That was a very simple psychological test, gentlemen— and one that is almost infallible. A true and a false memory cannot be distinguished by the mind. Bolton undoubtedly knew he had a dangerous problem. Whatever guilty facts I had mentioned, he also must mention. To have ignored guilty facts would have been a confession that he recognized them as guilty.

"Dale had no guilty memories at all to confuse him. He had no problem except to try and remember what I had read. He said starlight—got it mixed with moonlight. It generally is mixed on a clear night. He forgot the blue cap—just remembered something blue. He forgot the bench on which they were sitting. That was reasonable. A bench is unusual on a bridge. As a matter of fact, there is no bench on that bridge.

"I wanted to make sure of refreshing the guilty memories in this murderer's mind, and confusing those guilty memories with the memory of what I had read. You recall that faint, mysterious clanking sound a while ago, which we all ignored! It meant nothing to the innocent Thomas Dale.

"It was my simulation—in an adjoining room here— of the sound of the gears shifting the railroad semaphore signals which are on the bridge. We knew the murderer must have heard those gears shift as the train approached. They make quite a racket, and he and Mackenzie were sitting on the gear box.

"And the articles on that table," the Psychologist continued, "most of them were meaningless. To the innocent Dale, that little blue cape lying beside Alice's doll probably looked like a doll cape. But to the murderer it was a little garment for the coming baby. Mackenzie had it in his hand—they found it still clutched in his dead fingers. Evidently he had brought it to appeal to this seducer.

"Bolton recognized it on the table. And when I said blue cap—Mackenzie owned no blue cap—it was almost inevitable that Bolton should confuse the memories and think that I said blue cape. And he was the only one who knew of the coming child. The autopsy showed it, but the fact was never mentioned.

"He garbled my sentences on that point—got my words almost all correct—but out came his guilty knowledge of the child when I had said something wholly different! And Mackenzie was pushed through the rail, not over it! And in the deep railroad cut, the moonlight did not penetrate. Bolton—staring down at his victim—had an inescapable memory of the body, bathed not by moonlight, but by the headlight of the advancing train!

"Guilty memories, gentlemen, are the murderer's greatest danger. It's almost impossible for him to hide them—if you dig for them in scientific fashion."

X, THE MURDERER

THE VALET RAPPED lightly on his young master's bedroom door. It was eight o'clock, Sunday morning. The valet, a slim, dapper man of forty, with smooth-shaven face and close-clipped iron-gray hair, balanced a breakfast tray on the palm of one hand and knocked with the other. Receiving no answer to his second knock he called softly: "Mr. Eldridge—time to wake up, sir."

Still no answer. He went in. The young master's bed was rumpled but contained no sleeper. The valet laid his tray on the bed.

"Mr. Eldridge, sir," he called. Still no answer.

The valet looked into the adjoining room, a boudoir formerly occupied by young Eldridge's wife, now separated from him and living in another part of the big house. It, too, was empty, and the valet went on to the big bathroom.

"Mr. Eldridge, sir."

The bathroom was an unusual chamber, one of the several exotic features of this mansion which the gay young scion of the famous Eldridge fortune had built for his young bride three years ago. The entire room was black-tiled. A Roman bath occupied the full ten-foot width at the end of it, square-sided and sunk to a depth of six feet. It was quite possible to swim in it for a stroke or two.

"Mr. Eldridge—"

And then the valet saw. "Good God—"

A ladder of four or five steps led straight down into the bath. At the bottom, immersed in water, lay a nude body. It was caught between the ladder and the tiled side, securely wedged beneath a steel support to which the ladder was hooked. One of its arms seemed to have become entangled in the bottom step. The face goggled up at the valet, grotesquely blurred by the water. The mouth gaped.

Footsteps sounded in the hall, stopped. Dr. Johns, passing to the stairs on his way down to breakfast, had heard the valet's shouts. The door of a bedroom opened and Bob Berwin, Mrs. Eldridge's brother, came quickly out. He, too, had heard.

"What's up?" he asked.

"I don't know," the distinguished physicist replied. "It's coming from the big bathroom. Come on."

Another figure appeared on the stairs—John Appleton, Mrs. Eldridge's lawyer, here to arrange for her legal separation. Nanette Eldridge was with him; they had been walking in the garden when the valet's shouts had reached them.

Dr. Johns got to the bathroom first. He found the valet trying to haul out the body. He lent a hand and between them they managed to get it laid out on the sloping side of the pool. Someone had already telephoned for the family physician. It was useless. The body was stiffening.

"Dead several hours," the Physicist said. "Was he in the habit of taking baths in the dead of night?"

No one answered. Nanette Eldridge, who had become hysterical, had been taken to another room. The others

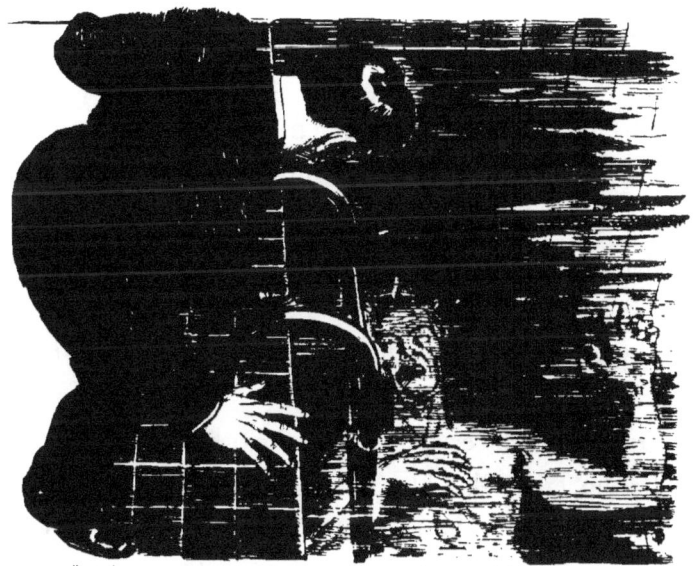

The face goggled up at the valet,
grotesquely blurred by the water.

were dumbfounded. Young Eldridge—dead—and accidentally drowned!

"There's something down in the water there," the Physicist said. "Do you see it, Thompson?"

The valet nodded. "I'll get it, sir." He went down the ladder, ducked under and brought up a man's heavy gold ring, set with a large solitaire diamond.

"Eldridge's," said Bob Berwin. "He always wore it."

John Appleton, who had led the dead man's wife from the room, came back. He confirmed Bob Berwin's statement.

Bob Berwin said: "The ring must have dropped from his finger. He went down after it ducked under, got confused, struck his head perhaps, and drowned."

"Do you think so?" asked Dr. Johns.

"Why, yes. Don't you?"

Dr. Johns shook his leonine head.

"Send for the police," he said. "This was murder."

IN THE GRILL room of the Scientific Crime Club, at nine o'clock that same Sunday morning, the Very Young Man sat alone, eating his breakfast. An attendant approached with a portable telephone, plugged it in. "Call for you, sir," he said.

The Very Young Man took it. "Hello. Jack Bruce speaking."

Dr. Johns's voice replied from the other end.

"Hello, Jack. Glad I located you. I'm out at Valley Hills, spending the weekend at the home of young Thomas Eldridge. Young Eldridge was murdered last night—"

"Is it a case for our club?" the Very Young Man cut in eagerly.

"I'm making it one," came the startling answer. "I've got to. I happen to be accused of the murder."

"Stop kidding," the Very Young Man said.

"I wish I were, Jack. The police are here, and all the evidence they've dug up so far seems to point nowhere else but at me. No, I haven't been arrested yet. I called Judge Malloy—he's the county judge and a friend of mine—he's coming over—meantime he's instructed the police to hold their horses.

"Anyway, here's what I want you to do. Round up some of our colleagues and get them over here. I think I can show them something interesting."

"The murderer?" asked the Very Young Man. "Do you know who did it already?"

"I know nothing," the Physicist responded emphatically. "Somebody here did it and I'm going to find out who,

simultaneously demonstrating a certain scientific principle to my conglomerate audience of criminologists, cops,
plain and fancy citizens, and one murderer. I'll want certain
apparatus. Listen closely. Bring your bathing suit—"

AT ELEVEN O'CLOCK that morning, the big, black-
tiled bathroom in the palatial home of the dead Thomas
Eldridge presented an odd scene. The ten-foot black pool
at its end had not been disturbed. The body still lay on the
sloping side, covered with a sheet. Along one wall near
the door, a dozen small chairs stood in a row. Six members
of the Scientific Crime Club occupied them. The local
police sergeant and his captain filled out the row, with two
uniformed members of the force. The Very Young Man was
the penultimate figure, and lastly, in a chair a little apart,
sat Judge Malloy.

At a right angle were five other chairs. The Physicist
occupied one. Beside him sat the little gray-haired valet,
Thompson. He had got wet hauling up the body and was
in a bathrobe now; his wet clothes were in a little pile on
the sloping side of the pool. Next to him was young Bob
Berwin, stalwart, smallish, dark-haired. The flabby John
Appleton sat beside him; at the end of the line was Nanette
Eldridge, her pretty pale face.

"What's this all about?" John Appleton asked. "This
scene—this stage-setting?" The lawyer had evidently been
holding himself in. "It strikes me as a highly unseemly
procedure, here in the very presence of death, to—"

"I have some evidence to present to the police," Dr. Johns
interrupted. "Unseemly? I have been accused of murder,
and I find that highly unseemly."

"Come now, gentlemen," Judge Malloy said. "No arguments. Captain Francis has agreed to let Dr. Johns present his evidence in his own way. I have no more idea of what the evidence is than you have. But I have great respect for the Scientific Crime Club, of which Dr. Johns is a distinguished member. I admit that the present procedure is extraordinary. But Dr. Johns has persuaded me that this pool cannot be left unguarded without risking the destruction of crucial evidence. You may proceed, Dr. Johns."

The Physicist stood up. Outwardly calm, he was inwardly agitated.

"I was the first to recognize this as a case of murder," he began—

"What made you think so?" the police sergeant interrupted. "You haven't told us that. Sure—a murder can be spotted as murder—by the murderer. Who should know better than he? I found out for myself pretty damn quick it was murder. I didn't need you to tell me.

"Look, Judge, I got here at 8:25 this morning. I found everybody excited; the body was lying where it is now. I was shown a man's diamond ring. It was the victim's. I was told it had been found lying on the bottom of the bathtub pool, under the steps. That suggested that death was accidental. But everybody seemed to assume it was murder. When I asked why, everybody looked at Dr. Johns. When I put it up to him, he wouldn't talk."

The sergeant glared belligerently at the Physicist.

"My explanation would have confused you, Sergeant," Dr. Johns said. "Besides, I wasn't ready to prove what I would have said. I'm ready now."

"Lemme finish," the sergeant said. "Thompson, the valet

here, was in a bathrobe like he is now. His wet clothes were lying over there—"

"Dr. Johns made me undress," the valet said. "He wrung out my wet clothes and wouldn't let anyone touch them."

"That's what they told me," the sergeant cut in. "I asked Dr. Johns why, but he wouldn't explain that either."

"I will in a moment," the Physicist said, "if you'll give me a chance."

"Wait a minute," the sergeant retorted. "I started my investigation. These five people here were the only ones in the house. The servants had leave. If it was murder— this was my line of reasoning—there was no evidence of anyone breakin' in here. The family doctor came. We established the cause of the victim's death—drowning. He gives it as his expert opinion that it happened not long after midnight. Somebody sneaked in here—shoved Eldridge down under that little ladder—"

FROM THE CRIME Club group the Astronomer interrupted: "How the devil do you know all that, Sergeant?"

"Don't interrupt him," Dr. Johns said. "It's true."

"You ought to know," the sergeant snapped. "You were the last person to see the victim alive. You've admitted you were alone with Eldridge from midnight till about one a.m."

"I didn't admit it," Dr. Johns corrected. "I volunteered it."

"Everybody else in the house was asleep. "Nobody saw Dr. Johns come out. The next thing it was eight in the morning, and Thompson found the body."

"What were you doing here with Mr. Eldridge from midnight to one a.m.?" Judge Malloy asked curiously.

Dr. Johns masked his impatience. "I was here for the

weekend on a business matter. Rather technical, but I'll sketch it. I'd developed a new method of anesthesia—the use of a chloroform device to supplant the ether cone—"

"I was comin' to that," the sergeant burst out. "The chloroform—"

"Let me finish, please," the Physicist said. "Young Mr. Eldridge, despite his gay, playboy habits for which he was too well known, was interested in my discovery. I am not a wealthy man. Young Mr. Eldridge had intimated that he might provide the money I needed. We were discussing it last night. I was showing him my method of anesthesia—"

Judge Malloy began to look uneasy. Dr. Johns noticed it, noticed the sudden gravity of all his friends as well. The sergeant's voice broke in again, sharply.

"The smell of chloroform in the bedroom was obvious to me. Mr. Eldridge's bed smelled of it."

"I left my case of drugs and apparatus with Mr. Eldridge," Dr. Johns snapped. "Neither of us thought anything about it. The case was closed, on the bedroom table—"

"Yeah," said the sergeant. "It wouldn't be so easy to shove Eldridge into that pool an' drown him without makin' a commotion. He got drugged, put to sleep. He was carried to this bathroom, lowered quietly into the water, an' his ring was planted to make it look like an accident—"

"I believe that is actually what happened," the Physicist agreed quietly.

"You ought to know," the sergeant again said.

"It wasn't I, Sergeant."

"Then who?"

The intent club members murmured to each other. The pale widow and her dark-haired brother exchanged glances. Thompson, the valet, stared blankly at the pool. The flabby Appleton hitched awkwardly in his chair.

"Gentlemen," the Physicist began, "in a little while I think we shall be able to answer that question. Young Mr. Eldridge showed me this Roman pool last night. He was very proud of it. He told me he was a fair swimmer and often shoved himself back and forth, half an hour at a time, for exercise. He said he had developed an underwater turn, like a caged seal's. I mention this to show you why, when I saw his body apparently caught by accident beneath the ladder, it struck me as almost incredible.

"Mr. Eldridge also informed me that every evening the water was drained out and filled again by Thompson. The pool has an *overflow outlet*. Don't forget that fact. The water stands normally at a depth of *exactly* six feet. The incoming flow continues until the six foot depth is reached. At that point the water escapes into the overflow. This automatically shuts off the incoming water so that there is no danger of a flood through carelessness. And no more water will enter the pool until someone again turns on the faucet! Is that correct, Thompson?"

"Yes, sir, quite correct," the valet said.

"And did you fill the pool last evening, Thompson?"

"Yes, sir, I did."

"At midnight," the Physicist resumed, "I saw that the pool was filled. This morning, when we found the body—" He paused. "My demonstration will be clearer than my words can be." He gestured to Jack Bruce. The Very Young Man, left his seat and came forward.

"Shall I put on my bathing suit, Dr. Johns?"

"Please, Jack."

The Very Young Man left the room. The Physicist resumed:

"Each one of us who was in the house last night had an equal opportunity to commit this murder—"

Appleton and Bob Berwin exclaimed with angry protest.

Judge Malloy said sharply: "Silence, please. You have not been accused. Go on, Doctor."

"Thank you. Now I want each one of us to be weighed. You, Judge Malloy, will please make a memorandum of our weights." He gestured to the nearby bathroom scales. "I'll start with myself. Captain, will you and the sergeant come and weigh me?"

He stood on the scales, with the police captain and the sergeant beside him. "We'll make whatever allowance is agreeable to you both for our clothing," he said. "Judge Malloy will note the net weights."

The weighing process over, the Judge read from his pencilled notes:

"Weights without clothing: Dr. Johns, 185; Mr. Berwin, 130; Mr. Appleton, 145; Wallace Thompson, 125; Mrs. Eldridge, 90."

THE VERY YOUNG Man appeared in his bathing suit. He carried a large metal container whose vertical sides were marked with circular rings. It was a measure for liquids.

"Captain," said Dr. Johns, "will you please weigh the container—empty?"

"Ten pounds," the captain announced in a moment.

"Now will you fill it to the top ring with water and weigh it again? You may use the footbath faucet across the room."

The captain filled the container.

"That water is the same as the water that goes into the pool, isn't it, Thompson?" the Physicist inquired.

The little valet was staring as if fascinated. "Yes, sir, of course."

"One hundred and thirty-five pounds," the captain announced when he and the sergeant had struggled with the container to the scales.

"Yes," the Physicist agreed. "Water weighs approximately sixty-two and one-half pounds per cubic foot. My container holds two cubic feet. You will notice it is graduated to register not the usual quarts and gallons but the poundage. Do you want to verify the container's accuracy any further, Captain?"

"No," the captain said. "Go ahead."

"Very well, then. The bathtub pool was filled last night by its automatic mechanism, filled to that narrow gold line which marks the six-foot depth. You see now that the water is below the line? Where did that missing water go to? Out through the overflow vent! What made it go? Jack—if you please."

The big container had been emptied into the footbath. The Very Young Man seized it. He affixed a little tin gadget to the overflow vent. The gadget was designed to prevent the overflowing water from escaping down the drain. At the same time it could divert it into the container.

"Get weighed, Jack," the Physicist ordered.

The Very Young Man obeyed. "One thirty-two pounds," the captain reported.

The Very Young Man went down the ladder into the pool and drew himself to the bottom with his head completely immersed. Only the splashing of the rising water as it went out the overflow into the container broke the silence in the room.

"His body is displacing the water," Dr. Johns informed the assemblage. "The human body, on the average, weighs 89 percent of an equal volume of water. Whether the lungs are expanded or deflated makes but a slight difference."

The Very Young Man had been under the surface a full minute. The water had taken less than half that time to spill into the overflow.

"Observe, gentlemen," the Physicist said, "that the ladder is at the opposite end from the overflow. Any ordinary splashing dies away before it travels the length of the pool. No water was lost that way—especially since the victim was drugged—no fight took place here in the water. Now we shall weigh the water Mr. Bruce has displaced."

There was a stirring of excitement now. Perhaps some of those present were beginning to see the goal toward which this strange demonstration was leading.

"What difference how much water Bruce displaced?" John Appleton asked sharply.

Dr. Johns disregarded him. "The little water clinging to the bathing suit is negligible," he said. "I have been very careful, at all times, to see that no appreciable amount of water escaped from the pool. For example, Thompson's clothes were wet when he hauled out the body this morning. I squeezed the water out of them, back into the pool."

"The water Mr. Bruce displaced weighs one hundred seventeen and one-half pounds," the police captain announced.

"That, gentlemen," the Physicist declared at once, having

made the simple calculation in his mind, "is just about 89 percent of his body weight of one hundred and thirty-two."

HE PAUSED, GLANCED at his fellow club members, smiled wryly. "Gentlemen, I come now to the crucial test. I *know* I am innocent. You, however, do not. My object in all this is to find the weight of the water missing from the pool—"

His voice had sharpened with inward excitement. He waited as the Very Young Man and the police captain carried the big container of water from the footbath and emptied it into the pool, going back at once for more.

"One hundred and twenty-five pounds," the captain said.

But the pool surface was still well under the narrow gold line. They poured in the second container.

"Two hundred and fifty pounds," the captain said.

Still more was needed. They came with a third container. But the pool would not take it all.

"Enough!" the captain said. He gazed at the figures on the container. "We've just added seventy-six and six-tenth pounds. Just about that—a total of three hundred twenty-six and six-tenths."

"Very well," the Physicist said. Two spots of color glowed in his cheeks and something very like triumph showed in his eyes. "We have left now only a simple mathematical problem," he announced. "A very simple one. I'll start you off on it, and you can finish it for yourselves by mere mental arithmetic. Let X equal the murderer! X was under the water. He was totally immersed, arranging the drugged body of his victim, holding his victim there until life was gone.

"Let X, in another sense, a more definite sense, equal the murderer's body weight. The victim was also immersed. The victim weighs 112 pounds. 89 percent of that is the weight of the water his body displaced. That's what his immersion caused to go out the overflow. 89 percent of 112 is 99.68 pounds of water. I deduct that from the total displaced water—326.6 minus 99.68. That leaves 226.92 pounds. That gentlemen, represents the water the *murderer* displaced. *It is 89 percent of the murderer's body weight!*"

The Physicist scribbled on a bit of paper. "226.92 pounds is fractionally close to 89 percent of 255 pounds. Read those body-weights again, Judge Malloy."

The judge obliged. "Dr. Johns, 185; John Appleton, 145; Mrs. Eldridge, 90; Mr. Berwin, 130; Wallace Thompson, 125." He looked up in bepuzzlement, shaking his head. "Why, Dr. Johns," he said, "this doesn't seem to get us anywhere. It would indicate that the murderer's body-weight was 255—and—and—"

"Figure it out," the Physicist said quietly.

Judge Malloy clapped a hand to his head. "I have it!" he fairly shouted. "There were *two!* Two weights on this list—one hundred and twenty-five and one hundred and thirty—equal to two hundred and fifty-five!"

The black-tiled bathroom rang with commotion. And underneath it a still, small voice murmured, "My God—my God!" It was the valet, the blood draining from his face.

Bob Berwin was the only one who had not moved. But now he swung in his chair and rasped in an undertone, "Shut up, you fool!"

But the Physicist had heard. "Thompson's silence won't save you," he said.

The police sergeant had leaped at Thompson. The little valet went suddenly and completely to pieces.

"We did it!" he screamed in a high, womanish voice. "Oh, my God!"

Berwin jumped for him.

"He wants to confess and you don't," the captain roared, and gripped Berwin. "Go on, Thompson—"

The valet had collapsed into a chair, sobbing. Words came from him with a rush.

"Yes—we did it. I've been sorry—God knows I've been sorry for my part in it—all night I've been praying God to forgive me. He—Mr. Eldridge—promised to marry my girl. She's only seventeen. Then he broke his promise and broke her heart. She committed suicide.

"Berwin knew how I felt. Yesterday he came to me with his scheme. He knew two of us would be needed to do away with Mr. Eldridge quietly. We found him asleep—three o'clock this morning. I thought I hated him for what he'd done to my girl—but I didn't hate him after I saw him lying there dead, with me a murderer. We drugged him with the chloroform while he slept—"

The miserable valet buried his head in his hands.

THE VOICE OF John Appleton came coldly.

"I happen to know that Berwin purloined Mrs. Eldridge's jewels, that he forged checks on her personal account, and on one of Eldridge's accounts. Eldridge had found it out and had threatened to jail Berwin."

The flabby lawyer shook his head sadly. "Berwin was the chief cause of the quarrels between Mr. and Mrs. Eldridge. It was my professional duty to arrange the separation, but I assure you I had no heart for it. I think that the whole thing was damn pathetic. I think if it hadn't been for Bob Berwin, Nanette's brother, she and her husband could have got on."

The captain manacled the glowering Berwin and took him out. Dr. Johns supported the trembling valet.

"The law may deal leniently with you," he said gently. "I'm a father—I have a girl—I understand."

He shook hands with the Very Young Man and with the other club members.

"Murder will out," he murmured, receiving their congratulations. "Even though it sometimes takes arithmetic and physics to bring it out."

www.ingramcontent.com/pod-product-compliance
Lightning Source LLC
Chambersburg PA
CBHW070222030726
47505CB00006B/1781